Serial Killers

Exploring the Horrific Crimes of Little Known Murderers

Jack Smith

Disclaimer

Disclaimer and Terms of Use: Effort has been made to ensure that the information in this book is accurate and complete. However, the author and the publisher do not warrant the accuracy of the information, text, and graphics contained within the book due to the rapidly changing nature of science, research, known and unknown facts, and internet. The author and the publisher do not hold any responsibility for errors, omissions, or contrary interpretation of the subject matter herein. This book is presented solely for motivational and informational purposes only.

Contents

Introduction

One of the strangest, most terrifying, and most fascinating aspects of our society is the existence of serial killers. There is an important distinction to be made between mass murderers and serial killers. The mass murderer commits multiple murders on one occasion, whereas the serial killer will murder on more than a single occasion and at different places. While murderers have existed for many centuries, the term serial killer is a contemporary construction. Many attribute the first use of the term to FBI agent Robert Ressler during a lecture he gave in 1974 in England. From an historic point of view, the first recording of serial killers can traced back all the way to Jack the Ripper, who terrorized women of the night in nineteenth century London. At the time, these brutal murders became front-page fodder for the newly popular newspaper industry. With people craving information about even the most horrifying of deaths, the idea of a killer addicted to murder was born. Since then, thousands of individuals have taken on the mantle of "Serial Killer," feeding into society's fascination with these strange and brutal people.

From John Wayne Gacy to Jeffrey Dahmer, many of America's most famous murderers have entered into the collective cultural consciousness. They have become pop culture figures, famous for their crimes and the violent nature of their acts. People feel compelled to understand more about these dark and twisted crimes, even when they disgust. For audiences everywhere, the very idea that these people can exist and operate in day-to-day life becomes an issue of abject terror and interest. That your neighbor, your boss, or your gas station attendant might be in the midst of a killing spree taps into something primal and very hard to imagine. It reflects the darkest side of the human psyche.

"Serial Killer" as a term can be difficult to define. Different criminal investigation units typically require two, three, or more attributable killings over a period of time before an individual can be considered to have joined the ranks of the serial killers. However, it is not really the numbers which can interest so many people and scare others. Instead, it is the often random nature of the killings. Rather than crimes of passion, crimes of financial reward, or instances when an individual has reached their end of their emotional tether, the crimes of serial killers have often been planned days, weeks, or months in advance. Targets can be random, but the killings are often planned in great detail. From cannibalism to mental health concerns, from ritualistic witchcraft to a simple interest in violence, learning what motivates these people can offer both insight and further confusion.

It speaks volumes that for every serial killer operating at any point in the world the amount of film, television, and literature focused on fictional versions is huge. From Hannibal Lecter to Patrick Bateman, these figures are often disguised metaphors for our own culture or the ways in which we interpret and react to the horrors of their real life equivalents. Serial killers, both real and fictional, are big business. They are reported on the news, make the front page of papers, and in films, which often, when based on their lives, top the box office. If there is one quality that is shared by all serial killers, it is the fact that we as a society are fascinated and appalled in equal measure.

With that in mind, anyone who has spent time looking into the subject probably knows everything there is to know about the typical rogues' gallery of mass murderers. Ted Bundy, Gary Ridgway, and Harold Shipman have all been front page news in America, the United Kingdom, and beyond. Their actions have become infamous because of their nature. But they are not alone. One former member of the FBI, John Douglas, suggested that there could be as many as thirty-five serial killers active at any one time in the United States alone. Expand these figures globally and some of the most monstrous murderers of all can sneak under the radar. In this book, we will take a look at some of the lesser-known serial killers, looking beyond the pale of conventional knowledge and discovering more about what drives these individuals towards such heinous acts. Read on and learn more about some of the most violent, chilling, and captivating individuals to have ever existed, history's hidden serial killers.

The isolated loner who butchered women and scattered their remains across Alaska

Robert Hansen

Also known as the Butcher Baker"

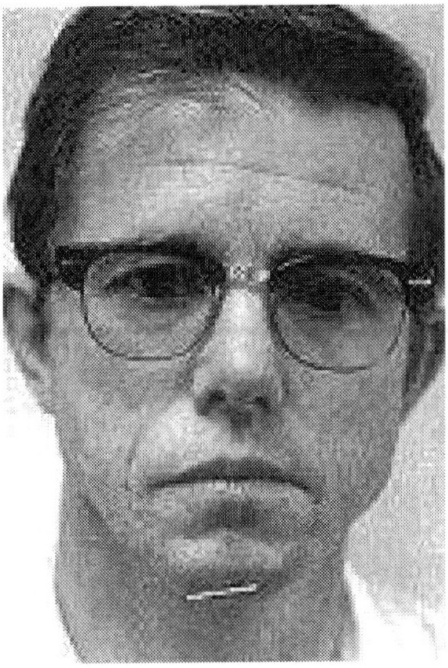

The setting

For many people, understanding the mind of the serial killer depends on being able to understand their childhood. For those who might think an upbringing of rejection and resentment helps create these individuals, the case of the Butcher Baker might be the archetypal example.

Robert Hansen was born in 1939 in Esterville, Iowa. His parents had recently emigrated from Denmark, and the young Robert was destined to step into his father's profession as a baker. Those who knew him as a child described Robert as "painfully shy;" his skinny frame, stutter, and severe bout of ace left him scarred physically and emotionally. His appearance meant he was shunned by the more attractive members of the opposite sex, forging a resentment which boiled and bubbled beneath the surface of Hansen's character. Increasingly dysfunctional and isolated, his relationships with family members – his father in particular – became strained. A victim of bullying and without the familial support others might have enjoyed, Robert Hansen took to hunting. It gave him a relief from his circumstances. He became quite the talented marksman. With this in mind, he enlisted himself in the Army Reserves, serving for one year before being discharged from the military. Similar positions as a police academy assistant drill instructor followed, during which time he met a young girl and fell in love. The pair married in 1960.

The first inklings of a darker side of Robert came to the fore in December of that year. After an arson attempt on a garage containing the local school bus, Robert was arrested and sentenced to twenty months of a three year stint in prison. His wife, not thinking this to be the man she married, sought to divorce her new husband. Robert served his time but, upon release, found himself alone again. He began to steal, serving minor prison sentences for petty theft. In 1967, having met another woman he intended to marry, they decided to move to Alaska. Now with two children in tow, the move to Anchorage seemed a shot at redemption for Robert, with his new neighbors admitting to warming to the man. He even managed to impress the locals with his hunting prowess, winning several awards for his marksmanship. He followed in his father's footsteps and became a baker. Everything seemed to be going well for Robert and his family, but it was not meant to last. During 1977, Robert was arrested and thrown in jail following the theft of a chainsaw. During this time, he was diagnosed by mental health professionals as having bipolar disorder. To combat this, he was given a prescription for lithium but was never under any official instructions to take the drug.

His crimes

Perhaps the most famous incident involving Robert Hansen (and the one about which we have the most detail) involves an attempted murder on June 13, 1983.

A young girl named Cindy Paulson managed to escape from a man who has been trying to shove her into the rear of his vehicle. Cindy, a seventeen-year-old, had been offered two hundred dollars to engage in a sex act with the man who had then drawn a gun on her and forced her to a home in the nearby area of Muldoon. Here, the man turned her into his captive. Cindy was repeatedly tortured, raped, assaulted, and kept chained to the wall by her neck while her captor slept. The man was Robert Hansen.

When her captor woke from his slumber, he stowed Cindy in his vehicle and drove to the nearby Merrill Field Aiport. Here, Robert informed his victim that they were to visit his 'cabin' – in actuality, this cabin was a meat shack near the Knik River which was only reachable using a boat or a small plane. This is when Cindy planned her escape. Bundled into the back seat of the car, her hands tied together, she was forced to wait until her attacker was no longer paying attention. As soon as her moment arrived, she crept out of the back seat and began to run, fleeing Hansen when his back was turned. At this point, she was not wearing her shoes. Crucially, she had decided to leave her sneakers behind in the back seat of the car. This would act as an indication to the police that she had indeed been held captive in the vehicle. Noticing his escaped captive, Hansen began to chase the girl. Before he could catch her, however, she had flagged down a passing truck and convinced the driver to pull over. With her disheveled and understandably terrified demeanor, the driver felt compelled to drive her to a local inn, wherein she pleaded with the front desk clerk to use their phone. She called her boyfriend while her savior – the truck driver – drove on to work. He would later inform the police of the incident.

Once the police arrived at Cindy's location, they were informed that she had telephoned a taxi and had driven to her boyfriend's place of work, a nearby motel. Officers found her there, handcuffed, afraid, and alone. She was taken to the local police headquarters and asked to make a statement. Details of her captor were given. Police who questioned Robert Hansen found that he denied any involvement, with the man suggesting to police that the girl was lying and possibly trying to extort him. Thinking Hansen not much more than a meek-mannered baker, and noting his confirmed alibi given by a friend, the police did not consider Robert Hansen to be a suspect in the kidnapping, rape, and torture of Cindy Paulson. Hansen was allowed to walk free.

At this time, Alaskan State Troopers had set up an investigation into the origin of a number of bodies discovered throughout the Anchorage area. These bodies had been found by locals and investigated by police, with many of the corpses never wholly identified. The lead investigator, Glenn Flothe, noticed the connection between the three killings and the similar manner of death in all three cases. Thinking there might be a killer on the loose, he requested additional assistance. Authorities constructed a psychological profile based on the recovered bodies, noting that the handiwork seemed that of an experienced and skilled hunter, one who might suffer from low self-esteem and who had been rejected in the past by the opposite sex. Particularly of interest was the killer's penchant for keeping "souvenirs" from each of his victims. These trophies included jewelry and other identifying marks. Perhaps most accurately of all, the profile even indicated that the killer might possess a stammer or stutter. Armed with this profile and the recent investigations into the capture of Cindy Paulson, Flothe began to work his way through the list. Eventually he worked his way to Robert Hensen, the experienced hunter with a stutter who owned a small plane.

The State Troopers obtained a warrant and searched Hansen's vehicles and home. As well as an arsenal of guns, they found several small items of jewelry, confirmed as belonging to the victims. One of the most important discoveries was a map hidden behind the suspect's headboard. Hansen has marked several small "x" notations all across the local countryside. Even though he was presented with a wealth of evidence, Hansen continued to deny any involvement. He blamed the women for trying to extort him and even tried to justify his actions. Finally, he confessed completely to a list of murders and the evidence presented to him. His list of victims even went back beyond the prostitutes and strippers who had led investigators to his capture, including sixteen- to nineteen-year-old girls who had not been found. Thanks to the one escaped victim and the work of the police, Robert Hansen was apprehended in 1983.

The Sentence

The first charges brought against Hansen were assault, numerous weapons citations, kidnapping, and even insurance fraud. This last charge related to the supposed theft of a number of his sporting trophies, the claimed insurance money having been put towards purchasing his vehicle. When speaking at his own trial,

Hansen recalled discovering the trophies at a later date but confessed that he did not inform the insurance company. The evidence against him began to mount up. Ballistics reports tied Hansen's weapons to the bullets found at numbers crime scenes. Eventually, Hansen entered a plea bargain. He admitted to his role in four killings of young women – those cases for which the police had evidence – and provided evidence leading to the discovery of the remains of his other victims. In exchange, Hansen would serve his time in a federal prison, and press attention would be restricted. Finally, he agreed to help decipher the small marks on the map found behind his headboard, helping grieving families locate their daughters' remains. Seventeen gravesites were located in all, a least a dozen of which had been unknown to the authorities. They covered a huge amount of South Central Alaska. Despite cooperation, there remained three notations on the map that Hansen would not reveal. The police suspect that these belonged to Mary Thill and Megan Emrick, killings in which Hansen denied any involvement.

Discussing his style of killing with the police, Hansen confessed to occasionally letting his victims go if they managed to convince him that they would not report him to the authorities. Tracing back his history of violence, he confessed that he had begun his murder spree as early as the start of the 1970s. The final sentence passed down from the judge was four hundred and sixty one years without the possibility of parole. While many of his victims' bodies have been recovered, the full extent of Robert Hansen's sadism has not been revealed. Despite over a decade of killing, his actions have largely escaped the collective cultural consciousness. This could be due to the remote Alaskan location or the plea bargain the serial killer struck. Perhaps it is encouraging to note the accuracy of the psychological profile constructed of the Baker Butcher, as Hansen was later known, and its importance in his capture.

The killer who hurled huge stones through his victim's heads

The Stoneman

Real identity unknown

The setting

In America, one of the chief advantages of the proliferation of investigative crime techniques is the increased success rate when dealing with serial killers. In many of the examples in this book, you will notice that police have caught their man using thorough and in-depth procedures. But these techniques are not global. In places such as India, the lack of investment and infrastructure needed to deal with these problems can cause major delays in catching the criminals. One killer who has remained elusive is known simply as The Stoneman.

As one of the most notorious killers in India's criminal history, it is perhaps shocking that more is not known about the individual's identity. This makes providing a background to the killer somewhat difficult. Instead, it can be important to have an understanding of the background of the case. Over the course of a two-year period, this person supposedly killed twelve homeless people while they slept. During this time, residents in Sion and Matunga areas were scared of leaving their home during the early hours. However, the primary target were those known locally as “rag-pickers” and other disenfranchised and vulnerable members of the community.

His Crimes

The key fact linking all of the killings was the manner of the murder. The Stoneman would use a large stone to crush the heads of his victims. Rather than repeatedly hitting a person over the head, many instances involved one large and heavy blow which was enough to crush the skull. Such a stone was found near many of the victims, and most weighed almost thirty kilograms. The victims would be those who were sleeping alone and out in the open of the streets. Each of the locations was chosen carefully by the killer so as to provide both privacy and a lack of potential evidence to leave behind. Starting abruptly, the killings ended in much the same fashion. After the local Stoneman murders ceased, very similar cases began in the city of Kolkata. Despite the clear links between the styles of murder in the two locations, police were still unable to trace any evidence linking the events. In spite of the lack of resources, authorities worked hard to put together various profiles of those they suspected.

The first involved a killer working under the instructions of a local spiritual leader. The ritualistic nature of the killings led some to believe there might be a religious element to the deaths. This was dismissed by some due to the brutal nature of the crimes, with the killer taking seemingly little ceremony beyond the actual act of killing.

The second profile was more in-depth. Police in Kolkata suggested that the serial killer would be a well-built man of taller than average height, the build required to repeatedly lift he murder weapons seemingly without effort. He would choose victims carefully and then kill them in such a manner that made identification almost impossible. Despite widening their net to include these suspicions, local police lacked the resources required to make their investigations more exhaustive. After a six month reign of terror, the Stoneman ceased in his killing.

The Investigation

No one was ever officially charged with the Stoneman murders. During the investigation and the initial crime wave, police rounded up many suspects and held them for a short time. During this period, the killings stopped.

But due to a lack of pressing evidence, police were forced to turn the men loose. Sniffer dogs were even brought in to find the killer, but the trail grew cold. While locals went as far as to blame supernatural forces, the true identity of the killer has never been exposed. While many serial killers are eventually caught and punished, India's Stoneman could be walking free to this very day.

Colombia's most violent serial killer

Luis Alfredo Garavito

Also known as The Beast

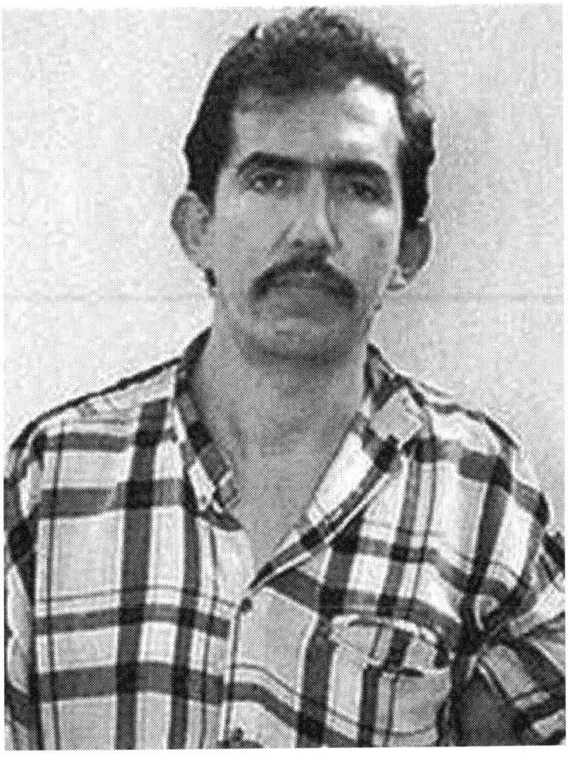

The setting

Luis Alfredo Garavito was raised in Colombia's coffee-centric region, Quindío. Born in 1957, he was the eldest of his family's seven sons. His father was a violent man and would occasionally beat the boys. Two of the family's neighbors reportedly raped the young Luis throughout his early years. Luis attended his local school for five years but left by the time he was sixteen, leaving his home behind as well. He found work as a clerk in a store and as a street vendor, selling religious items to passers-by. Embittered by his violent and devastating childhood, Garavito drifted from one job to the next, developing alcoholism. His drifting lifestyle involved arriving in a town, outstaying his welcome, and then moving on to the next. Having made at least one suicide attempt, he spent five years under psychiatric care.

His Crimes

The true nature of Garavito's crimes began was revealed in 1998. Two children's corpses were discovered outside of Colombian town of Genua. Stripped naked and lying next to one another, a search of the area turned up a third body, though the rate of decomposition indicated it had been left there for some time. On finding the bodies, authorities noticed they had each been bound at the wrist and the area was littered with blood stains. With a knife found nearby, the bodies had been mutilated, with particular attention paid to the children's necks and genitals. There were also signs of biting and of anal penetration. Despite the wealth of DNA evidence at the scene, lack of funding meant such investigative techniques were unavailable. Police had to begin their search elsewhere.

During this time, politically unstable Colombia was home to several known serial killers, including Pedro Alonso Lopez, who killed close to seventy people. Despite this, the deaths of the children matched nothing else known in the country. The children were identified and traced to a local town. They were close friends and had grown up together in a poor environment. Aged eleven and thirteen, they sold items on the streets to add to their family's meager incomes.

One of the victim's mothers was able to provide additional clues. Her son had run home to tell her the boys were planning on helping a man move his cows. Despite their close relationship, the boys vanished on different days. Afterwards, the police deduced that Garavito would lure his young victims to a coffee shop with promises of cake. Here, he would assess their skin quality, their characters, and ask them various questions. Should they pass his test, he would then enlist them to help him with a task, such as moving cows. He even possessed various disguises to make the story convincing, such as a priest or a salesman. Each time, his intention was to lure the children away with promises of money or treats, convincing them to come quickly and not to return home before they left with him.

Having established a regular routine for the as-yet unidentified serial killer, the police began to look through past murders to try and find any correlation. Hundreds of cases of missing children had been reported, and among these were many cases of murdered children who couldn't be identified. It is thought that as many as twenty-seven of Garavito's victims have not been identified to this day. One particular spate of killings in 1995 in Valle seemed to target the same demographic of eight- to ten-year-old boys. All had come from similar backgrounds, and their parents reported similar circumstances around their disappearance. At the scene of the murders, the bodies had not been buried. Often, the same spot had been used multiple times. On arrival, children might become suspicious, but they were bound and then killed before they could escape.

One notable case involved a boy who vanished in 1996 outside of Boyaca. The boy rode his bicycle while following Garavito out of the town. His corpse was found some days later, the head decapitated, and his severed penis shoved in his mouth. A search conducted by the boy's mother led them to a man people had identified as having bought the boy sweets; Garavito. The police questioned him but were unable to deduce the true nature of the man in their custody. They released him, only for Garavito to kill another boy only four days later in a nearby town.

Due to quickly decomposing bodies, identifying exact wounds was often difficult. One repeated identifier was the attempted decapitations, with post mortems indicating that an old and rusty knife was used to try and cut the boys' heads off. On some occasions, Garavito would load the bodies into a sack with stones and dump them in a river. During the murders, the killer would often drink alcohol. A familiar sight at the scene was an empty bottle of cheap schnapps.

Armed with a wealth of evidence and finally realizing that this was the repeated work of one individual, authorities began to note a pattern to the still-unidentified killer's work. Garavito would divide his killing locations into sectors, limiting himself to only a few victims per sector before moving on. He would rotate among his favorite killing spots. At these isolated locations, the killer would tie up his victims, though he might allow them to stumble around. Many victims were raped, but it was unclear whether this was before or after their death. Typically,

Garavito would kill during weekends. At this time, children would be gathered in the markets. Luring them away during this time raised less suspicion and allowed him to blend into the crowds. Parents might assume their children were off playing while instead they had been taken to one of the killer's murder scenes.

The sheer volume of murders conducted by Luis Alfredo Garavito during this time meant many members of the public were unwilling to accept that all of the murders were committed by one man. Many blamed local Satanists or cults instead. As the police finally managed to put together a pattern, the actions of the serial killer became more and more apparent. Even as he was terrorizing the young boys of Colombia, many were unable to comprehend the scope of his actions.

The Sentence

The breakthrough in the case came in 1999. At this time, a homeless man witnessed the attempted rape of a young boy by an adult man. Taxi drivers in the area ratified the story, matching the descriptions of the man. The name given by the suspect was the name of a politician in a nearby town – clearly a lie. Garavito, walking along a road, was arrested. Though he protested that he was simply walking to a nearby town, his matching physical description was enough to place him in jail while the authorities investigated.

During this time, agencies across the country attempted to merge their information. In a per-internet or digital age, this was incredibly difficult. The political events in Colombia at the time made consistent law enforcement difficult. A collaboration with national and international police forces allowed for extra manpower to uncover the extent of Garavito's crimes. The suspect's Armenian heritage meant representatives from that country were drafted in to help.

Luis Garavito confessed to the murders of one hundred and forty children. In addition, he has been charged with killing an additional thirty young boys. The court found him guilty of one hundred and thirty nine of these murders, though investigations continue to this day. Garavito is still able to provide locations and draw maps for authorities. His prison sentence is limited to thirty years due to local laws, but his co-operation has lowered this number again to twenty-two. To this day, Garavito remains in Colombian jail, though the day for his potential release draws ever closer.

The police investigator who was secretly a serial killer

Serhiy Tkach

Also known as The Pologovsky Maniac

The setting

Even those killers with the highest number of murders attributed to them can be comparatively less famous. One such example is Serhiy Tkach, the Pologovsky Maniac, who has been accused of over one hundred murders in his native Russia. While many serial killers are methodical thinkers who elude police detection, Serhiy Tkach was a police investigator himself. He knew all the tricks of the police, allowing him to remain a step ahead of the law up until he was caught. His crimes occurred in both Russia and Ukraine, remaining free of suspicion thanks to his knowledge of police procedures.

His Crimes

Serhiy Tkach's was known for being selective about his victims. He selected girls between the ages of eight and eighteen. He would suffocate them before raping their corpses. It is unknown when he began to kill, though many suggest that his move to Ukraine in 1982 was the first time he was documented as having killed. Despite this, many suspect his crimes trace back to Siberia and began as early as 1980. The difference between the number of murders he was charged with and the number of crimes to which he has confessed means that identifying his actual victims is almost impossible.

Despite this, we do know that his killing spree lasted as long as twenty-five years. For a quarter of a century, others were arrested for the crimes he had committed, since his careful ability not to leave behind clues made his deeds incredibly tough to investigate. Thanks to the time he spent in the police force, he was able to sweep a crime scene and remove anything that might link him to the murder. His eventual mistake was being caught in the company of a friend's daughter. Witnesses recall seeing Tkach talk to the girl who would later be found murdered. Police were finally led to his door.

The sentence

Delving deeper into the myriad of crimes committed by Serhiy Tkach, authorities eventually charged him with twenty-nine murders and a further eleven cases of attempted murder. Knowing himself to be caught, Tkach confessed to a further hundred murders and demanded the death penalty for himself. However, the collapse of the Soviet Union meant such a punishment was no longer in place, and instead he was sentenced to life in jail.

Because of his punishment, Serhiy Tkach has been interviewed on numerous occasions for those searching for information about why he committed his crimes. Initially, he would suggest that revenge was the main motivation behind the murders, as he remarked that women (especially his three wives) had mistreated him during his life. This explanation eventually gave way to a confession that he derived sexual pleasure from the act and that it allowed him to gain an intellectual victory over his former police colleagues.

One interesting aside is the fact that others were charged for his murders. Having gone so far as to imprison some of these men, Serhiy Tkach's eventual capture and confession meant that they were later released and absolved of their crimes. While we do not know how many murders he committed exactly, his skill at evading capture led to others being caught, tried, and charged in his place.

The woman who murdered hundreds of adopted babies

Amelia Dyer

Also known as The Ogress of Reading

The setting

While we have traced the lineage of the serial killer back to men such as Jack the Ripper, there are those who have been lost to history and those who are frequently overlooked when discussing these crimes. One such woman was Amelia Dyer. Unlike many who were born in 1837, Dyer was not raised in abject poverty. Instead, she was the youngest of five, raised in the town of Pyle Marsh, just outside the South West English city of Bristol. Her father was a skilled shoe maker, and the family were relatively well-off. During her upbringing, Dyer developed a love for literature of all sorts. Despite the financial cushion of her childhood, her mother's mental health issues brought about by typhus caused distress. Dyer cared for her mother through the violent fits and the hallucinatory episodes until the old woman passed away in 1848. For many biographers, this was a watershed moment in Amelia Dyer's life.

Following her mother's death, Dyer left to live with her aunt in the nearby city. She began a career as an apprentice corset maker. Her father passed away in 1859, leading her eldest brother to inherit the shoe-making business. During this time, with Amelia in her mid-twenties, she began to grow increasingly estranged from her family. She met George Thomas, a man of fifty-nine, and married him. On their marriage certificate, he reduced his age and she increased hers, making their ages seem closer. This caused a great deal of confusion for later reporters.

Following her marriage, Dyer began to work as a nurse. In the Victorian time, this was a hard and grueling trade. During her period as a midwife, she began to learn about the young women who were about to give birth to illegitimate children. She would welcome these young girls into her home for a small sum before selling their children for adoption or taking care of them in exchange for cash from the expectant mothers. This practice, known as baby farming, would involve the practitioners building up a large number of babies, who would often starve or die from malnourishment. Alcohol and opium were used to subdue and quieten their demise. When George Thomas died, this would be the income Amelia turned to.

Her Crimes

Dyer learned about baby farming from Ellen Dane, who was forced to flee the country following her involvement in baby farms. In attracting potential girls into her home, Dyer assured them she was kind, caring, and would provide a loving home. After some time in the baby farming industry, Dyer began to hasten the process. Where others would allow babies to perish through malnourishment and a lack of care, Dyer simply killed them. This meant she would keep all of the expenses paid to her for the child's upbringing by the destitute mothers.

Despite the circling interests of the authorities, Dyer continued in her practice. She was almost caught after a doctor raised concerns after being asked to certify a number of deaths that had occurred in her care. Rather than being tried for murder, Dyer was sentenced for neglect and forced to complete six months' hard labor. This sentence would have a crushing effect on her mental well-being.

She was not away for long. After serving her sentence, Dyer attempted to resurrect her nursing career. However, she had to spend time in various mental health institutes after exhibiting instability and tenancies towards suicide. Thanks to her medical training, Dyer knew how best to interact with the staff to ensure a comfortable, if not pleasant, life. At one point, she was charged with caring for the baby of a local governess. When the mother became suspicious, she returned to the baby to check the child's one-of-a-kind birthmark.

There was no mark present on the baby. Dyer either suffered from or feigned a mental breakdown and even tried to drink two bottles of laudanum in a suicide attempt. Due to her time abusing the substance, her tolerance ensured she survived. Instead, she spent her time in and out of various facilities.

It was perhaps inevitable that she would return to her career as a baby farmer. This time, rather than having doctors certify the deaths, she began to dispose of the bodies of her own accord. Her actions remained suspicious, whether it was the police or the mothers who accused her of ill deeds. This forced Dyer to move constantly, taking on a number of aliases to escape detection. She recruited a girl called Jane Smith from a workhouse and, in tandem with Dyer's own daughter and son-in-law, began to present Smith as the caring face to young mothers seeking a future for their illegitimate child.

One of the only cases we have exact details about involves the death of Doris Marmon. Having advertised in a local paper, Doris was bought to Dyer and reluctantly left behind by her poor mother. Having received £10 for the child's care and upbringing, Dyer used a length of white tape, wrapped twice around the baby's neck, and chocked Doris until she died. She wrapped the body in a carpet bag, weighed it down, and tossed it into the Thames River. When the mother came to visit the child, she found Dyer had already left.

The sentence

It would be a similar murder which would lead to Dyer's capture. While moving down the river, a bargeman came across a package in the Thames. Inside was the corpse of a baby girl who was identified as Helena Fry. Despite limited resources, the detectives investigating the murder managed to find the label from a Bristol station and – thanks to a microscopic investigation of the wrapping paper which held the baby – uncovered the faint trace of a name and an address.

These details led detectives to Dyer, or at least, one of her aliases. Despite this link, the evidence was still not enough to convict the murderous baby farmer. Investigators began to interview witnesses and anyone associated with Dyer. These checked police records relating to their suspect and their suspicions grew. They knew Dyer might attempt to flee if she thought she was under suspicion, so they placed her under surveillance.

To gather the right evidence, the detectives decided to use a sting operation. They would bring in a decoy young girl and pretend to discuss the services Dyer was known to offer. When Dyer was expecting her fake client to arrive, she instead found that two detectives had come to greet her. They entered the house and were met by the stench of rotting bodies. Despite the smell, no bodies were found on the premises. Instead, they found other evidence, including the murder weapons, communications regarding potential clients, receipts for pawned children's clothes and letters from mothers worried about their babies.

Using this evidence, the police were able to deduce that Dyer had killed twenty babies in the preceding few months alone. At this rate, some suspect that she may have killed as many as four hundred babies over the course of her baby farming career. This would place Amelia Dyer as one of the most vicious serial killers of all time.

On April 4, 1896, Amelia Dyer was arrested. Investigators searched the Thames and found six further bodies. All of the victims bore the same strangulation marks, a technique Dyer later admitted was her signature method. Doris Marmon was one of the last bodies to be recovered from the river and was identified by her mother. Dyer was charged with murder, as was her family. Though the family was later acquitted, Dyer wrote a letter relieving them of all involvement.

Dyer was placed on trial at the Old Bailey and charged with one murder. She pleaded guilty. She recalled having escaped exposure on several occasions. Of the witness accounts, the most damning was that from a man who had seen her disposing of a body and of her own daughter, Jane. In her defense, Dyer offered her poor mental health history. These, the prosecutors argued, were staged attempts to remove suspicion. The jury found her guilty in less than five minutes. She was awarded the death penalty. While she sat in a cell, she wrote out her "last true and only confession." It took up five exercise books. These were offered to the visiting chaplain the night before she was to be put to death, with the question, "Is this enough?"

Amelia Dyer was hanged on June 10, 1896 at Newgate Prison. Her final words were "I have nothing to say." To this day, we are unsure of the exact number of babies she murdered. The number of mothers who asked about Dyer stretched into the hundreds. Causing a scandal, she was front page news. Song writers composed verses about her actions and her death. Despite the huge number of babies she killed, her position as a serial killer is often forgotten. As one of the most evil women in history, she has certainly done enough to become notorious.

A month-long killing spree from the former mental health patient

Richard Trenton Chase

Also known as the vampire of Sacramento

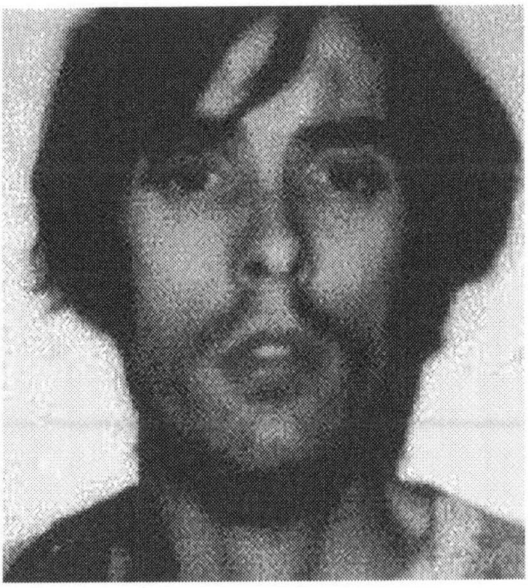

The setting

One of the most important traits for those investigating the motivations and childhoods of serial killers is the presence of certain triggers and warning signs. Those who are labelled serial killers often share similar psychological tics which manifest in childhood and continue into their adult life. One man who exhibited such traits was Richard Chase, otherwise known as the Vampire of Sacramento. Born in California, Chase's childhood was not a happy one. Beaten by his mother, he was known to exhibit what is now known as the Macdonald Triad. These are enuresis (a repeated inability to control urination), pyromania (an inability to fail to resist impulses to deliberately start fires), and zoosadism (pleasure derived from cruelty to animals).

As he grew into adulthood, he became dependent on alcohol and developed hypochondria. Chief among his complaints was a belief that his heart would frequently stop beating or the insistence that someone had taken away his pulmonary artery. He shaved his head in the belief that he could watch his skull shifting beneath the skin and believed he could absorb the vitamins of an orange through the palm of his hand.

He left home and moved in with friends. These people came to resent his frequent use of psychedelic drugs and reliance on drinking. Chase would also make his roommates uncomfortable by strutting around the house without clothes. After he refused to move out, everyone else left. At this point, Chase began to trap and kill animals in the home, often disemboweling his prey and eating their flesh raw. This, he suggested, stopped his heart from shrinking. In 1975, he was committed to a mental health ward. He told staff about his various fantasies about killing rabbits and even managed to capture, kill, and eat birds inside the facility. Over time, he developed the nickname "Dracula."

During his stay, he claimed to have drained blood from a therapy dog and frequently defecated in the ward, smearing his feces around the walls. This behavior eventually led to a diagnosis of paranoid schizophrenia. With a prescribed list of medicines, Chase was released into the care of his mother. Over the coming years, she began to ease her son off the medication and eventually found him an apartment. In the summer of 1977, Chase was stopped by the police. He was smeared with blood and had a bucket of even more blood in his truck. This was later found to be cow's blood, and he was released once again.

His Crimes

The first known murder at the hands of Richard Chase occurred on December 29, 1977. Ambrose Griffin was a father in his early fifties, shot down by a driver who sped away. Police investigated the local area but found no leads. After two weeks, Chase then attempted to gain entry to a locked home. Failing to get through the lock, he would later mention that locked doors were a signal of him not being welcome in a home. He was chased from one home after defecating on the bed and clothes of a couple. They chased him from their house, but he remained at large.

The next victim was a women named Teresa Wallin. A pregnant woman, Chase shot her three times while she was at at home. He then proceeded to rape the corpse, using a butcher knife to stab her during the act. Before he left, Chase took several organs, a nipple, and drank some of her blood. His final act was to remove dog feces from the lawn and to jam them down his victim's throat.

The final murders committed came at the end of January. Evelyn Miroth was entertaining Danny Meredith at her home when Chase entered. He shot them with his handgun and moved through the home, stealing wallets and car keys. Also in the house were Evelyn's son and nephew, aged six years and twenty two months respectively. He shot them both. As with Teresa Wallin, Chase engaged in sex acts with the body of the woman he had just killed. He was disturbed from this when there was a knock at the door. Evelyn's son was expecting a play date with a local six-year-old girl. She was at the door. Chase ran, taking the son's body with him. Finding no one home, the girl alerted a neighbor, and the police were called. When they walked into the home, they found Chase's bloodied handprints around the home. He was quickly tracked down.

The sentence

After being caught, Richard Chase was tried for six murders. In an attempt to avoid execution, Chase's lawyers suggested that his actions were second degree murders, a charge carrying a life sentence. With Chase's history of mental health issues, they felt his crimes were not of a premeditated nature.

The case received a huge amount of attention. On May 8, the jury returned a verdict of guilty on all counts of first degree murder. Chase would face the gas chamber. In jail, Chase's reputation preceded him. Other inmates were wary of their murdering cellmate. According to those working at the jail, some criminals imprisoned with him tried to convince Chase to kill himself.

The story does not end there. Chase allowed a reporter, Robert Ressler, to conduct a number of interviews. During these sessions, Chase shared his fears of alien invasions and Nazis. The murders, he suggested, were not his fault. Instead, they were acts of self-preservation, essential for him to continue living. He requested

Ressler obtain a radar gun on his behalf, to better fight the Nazi aliens, and handed the interviewer a large amount of pasta and cheese which he had been keeping in his pocket. He suspected the guards were in league with his extra-terrestrial tormentors and were trying to kill him.

The day after Christmas, 1980, a guard checked in on Chase's cell. He was found lying awkwardly and was not breathing. He had committed suicide, with autopsy reports indicating he had been stockpiling prescribed anti-depressants in order to purposefully overdose. Despite his spree only lasting a month, Chase's position in the media and his recorded interviews gave the public a real insight into the mind of a serial killer.

The letter-writing cannibal of old New York

Albert Fish

Also known as the Werewolf of Wysteria

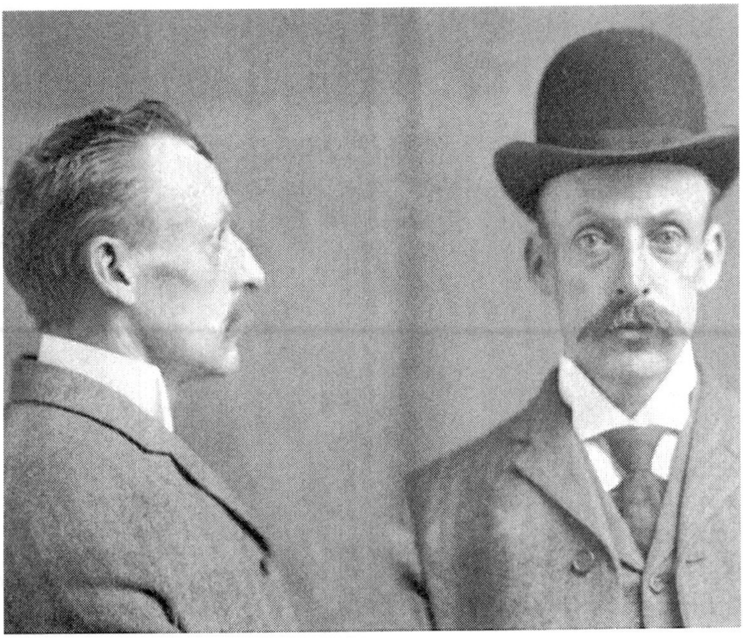

The setting

While Richard Chase became a household name in a short amount of time, the rise and fall of serial killers has not always been so rapid. During the nineteenth century, the ability for a murderer to go undetected for long periods of time allowed them to reach astonishingly high numbers of deaths. One such man was Albert Fish, born in Washington in 1870. Of English descent but thoroughly American, Fish was born to a mother who was forty-three years younger than his father. By the time Albert was born, his father was seventy-five. With a family history of mental health concerns, he was given up for adoption and spent many of his formative years in an orphanage. Here, he was given the hated nickname "ham and eggs." The treatment he received at St John's Orphanage has been described by some as "sadistic," with the young Albert Fish hurt so often that he would eventually come to enjoy the pain. In his own words, he was "mercilessly whipped."

At the age of ten, his mother was able to secure a job despite her health concerns, and she removed young Albert from the orphanage. Once released, Albert met a young telegraph boy and became friends. Together, then began to drink urine and eat feces. Fish began to attend public baths where he would be able to watch other boys as they undressed. Around this time, he began the practice of selecting women's names from classified adverts and writing to them with salacious and obscene letters.

His Crimes

At the age of twenty, he moved to New York. Here, in his career as a prostitute, Fish began to rape young boys. To ward off a growing reputation, his mother arranged for him to marry a women nine years younger than himself. Together they had six children, though Albert was far from an attentive parent. Over the next ten years, Albert Fish took on a job as a house painter, all the while continuing his practice of molesting and raping young boys. He spent time in jail, charged with grand larceny. He recalled one visit to a museum that contained a waxwork replica of a dissected penis which he claimed was "fascinating."

One of the most telling relationships Albert Fish forged was with a man known as Thomas Kedden, whom he met while working in Delaware. They met in 1910 and soon entered into a sadomasochistic relationship. Fish confessed he believed Kedden to have learning disabilities, and it is unclear how consensual the relationship truly was. Regardless of how it began, it would end violently. After knowing one another only ten days, Fish whisked Kedden away to an old house on a farmstead. Here, he began to torture Kedden. He bound his captive and sliced his penis in half, an act which he says prompted a scream Fish would "never forget."

Fearing he would be caught if he killed Kedden and disposed of the body, Fish instead doused the wound in peroxide and used Vaseline smothered on a handkerchief to wrap it up. He left Kedden a ten dollar bill, kissed him, and took to the road, taking the first train back to New York. Fish says he never knew what happened to Kedden.

At the start of 1917, Fish's wife began a relationship with another man. John Straube was a boarder with the family and left with Albert's wife, leaving Fish alone to raise his six children. As she left, his wife took with her all of the valuables, or so claims Albert. By this point, he was beginning to have increasingly strong hallucinations and believed himself to be communicating with the Apostle John. He also took to the practice of self-harm, shoving needles into his abdomen and groin. Doctors would eventually give him an x-ray, finding twenty-nine needles crammed into the pelvic region. He would also flagellate himself with a "nail-studded paddle" and insert lighter-fluid soaked wool into his anus before setting it alight. It is reported that Albert Fish was never violent towards his children but instead encouraged them to be violent toward him, requesting that they paddle and beat his rear end with the same paddle he used to self-harm. Coupled with this, a growing obsession with cannibalism meant Fish frequently served his children dinners of nothing but raw meat, a dish he would typically enjoy himself.

But his crimes had not ended. In 1919, he met and stabbed a boy who suffered from mental health concerns in Washington D.C. Usually, he selected either those with clear handicaps or African-American people as his victims, thinking that no one would miss them. His usual targets were children, and his favored tools were those of a butcher: a meat cleaver, a bone saw, and a large butcher's knife. He named these tools his "implements of hell."

He had several "near-victims." One such child was Beatrice Kiel, who Fish encountered while she was playing alone on a farm in Staten Island. He asked the girl to help him search for rhubarb and offered her money. Just as she was about to leave with him, her mother stepped out and chased Fish away. Unperturbed, he returned to the home and spent the night trying to sleep in their barn. He was discovered by the home owner and chased from the land again. Throughout this time, Fish began to sink deeper into his psychosis, believing ever more fervently that he was being commanded by God to kill and mutilate small children. Cyril Quinn was another near-victim, who Fish caught playing on a street with a friend. He invited the boys to his home for lunch. While the two wrestled, they came across Fish's murder weapons and immediately ran away.

In 1928, Albert Fish read a newspaper advert in which an eighteen-year-old Edward Budd sought employment. Under the guise of potentially hiring the young man, Fish went to the apartment in Manhattan. His plan, he later confessed, had been to torture and kill Edward Budd. After blustering through a story about a job, Fish left but visited the apartment again. He switched his target to Grace Budd, a family member whom he invited to a party. She agreed to go with Fish and was never seen again. Fish remarried in 1930, but his marriage to Estella Wilcox lasted only a week. That May, he was arrested after sending more obscene letters to women from classified adverts. Following this incarceration – and another a year later – he was sent for a psychiatric evaluation. He was released and continued to hunt, kill, rape, and mutilate.

In 1934, Fish anonymously posted a letter to the family of Grace Budd. This would become the single clue which led police to his door. In the letter, Fish told the story of a sailor, Captain John Davis, who travelled to China. Due to a famine in the country, people were selling human meat cut from young children. Forced to stay in the port a while, Fish claims that Davis became addicted to the taste of human flesh. These facts have not been verified and are likely untrue. Fish continues the story of Davis, telling of how he caught, imprisoned, killed, and cooked two young boys in America. Throughout the letter, Fish claims to have been Davis's neighbor, watching as the man committed the crimes. He then suggests that Davis caught and ate Grace in a similar manner but did not rape her, though he could have. He finishes the letter by commenting that "she died a virgin."

Unable to source the information in the letter regarding a Captain Davis or a cannibalistic Chinese port, the police were able to match the story of Grace Budd's death with the account given in the letter.

Because of the close matches between the account in the letter and the suspected death of Grace Budd, investigators made this the center of their case. On the envelope, there was a small symbol representing the New York Private Chauffeur's Benevolent Association. Chasing down this information, police were led to a janitor who claimed to have taken some of the stationary but had left it behind in a boarding house after moving out. They went to the landlord, who gave them the information for Albert Fish, who had just left the room a few days previous. The landlord also claimed that Fish's son had left some money for his father, and Fish had requested that she hold on to it a short while. The police monitored this closely, waiting for Fish to arrive back at the home.

When he arrived back at the room, Fish first agreed to be taken to the police station for questioning but then took out a razor blade from his pocket and threatened the arresting officers. Despite the weapon, police disarmed the man and took him away. Once in custody, Fish recalled the tale of how he had originally planned to kill Edward Budd but instead changed his mind. He even mentioned that it had "never even entered" into his mind to rape Grace, but on speaking to his attorney, Fish did confess to two "involuntary ejaculations" during the murder. This information, along with his confession, would form the bulk of evidence against him during a trial, used to claim a sexual motivation and avoiding mentioning the potential for cannibalism that had so obsessed Albert Fish.

The Sentence

The trial for the murder of Grace Budd took place in 1935. The judge was a man named Frederick P. Close, and he oversaw a court in White Plains, New York. In all, the length of the trial was just ten days. Albert Fish and his lawyers entered a plea of insanity, referencing the killer's belief in hearing instructions from God that he should kill children. Many psychologists were called to the stand, divulging information on the many fetishes and interests Fish possessed, including sadism, masochism, anilingus, flagellation, voyeurism, cannibalism, coprophagia, urophilia, and pedophilia. In mounting his client's defense, Fish's lawyer surmised that Albert Fish was a wholly unique "psychiatric phenomenon," and that his list of sexual abnormalities constituted the condition of a man who was not entirely sane.

A key part of the defense was the child psychiatrist Fredric Wertham, who gave two days' worth of testimony. During this time, he explored the religious obsession of Albert Fish, as well as the primary focus on the story of Abraham and his son. As in the biblical tale, Fish believed that sacrificing a child would provide atonement for his sins. Due to the lack of divine intervention during the murder of children, Fish took his actions to be correct in the eyes of God. Wertham even suggested that – in the case of Grace Budd – Fish had seen his victim not as a woman but as a young boy. He also commented on the cannibalism, linking it to the Christian practice of communion. After a lengthy question regarding Fish's entire life up to that point, the doctor surmised his evaluation by simply suggesting that Albert Fish "is insane."

The trial was perhaps one of the first to make extensive use of the still nascent science of psychotherapy and psychiatry. Many noted professors and doctors were called to the stand to give their verdict on Fish and whether he was truly insane or simply deluded. After the ten days of cross examination and medical hearing, the court found Albert Fish to be both sane and guilty. He would receive the death sentence.

This sentence was carried out on January 16, 1936 in the electric chair at Sing Sing prison. On the night before he died, Fish drafted one final letter. He handed several sheets of paper to his lawyer the next day and told him they were his final words and were to be distributed to the press. The day after the execution, the lawyer revealed his possession of the letters to the press but informed them that he would not reveal the contents to anyone, claiming them to be "the most filthy string of obscenities that I have ever read." After many years of murdering and eating young boys and other people, the serial killer known as Albert Fish was put to death, his last act of obscenity destroyed.

The killer tried inside an iron cage for the court's protection

Andrei Chikatilo

Also known as the Butcher of Rostov

The setting

Some people are included in this book because they show an often forgotten element of the serial killer psyche. Some are included for their historical importance. Some demonstrate how the police typically investigate serial killers. Andrei Chikatilo is included simply because he killed a large number of people in a very violent fashion.

Andrei Chikatilo was born into a country in the tragic depths of a famine. Farming policies laid out by Soviet leader Joseph Stalin had plunged Ukraine into crisis, leaving many without food. Millions died. Both of Chikatilo's parents were farm laborers. The family lived in a single-roomed hut. Due to the collectivized nature of their work, they received no wages but instead were allowed to work a plot of land near their home. This led to the family frequently going hungry, with Chikatilo himself later mentioning that he did not taste bread until he was twelve years old. Instead, he says the family often got by on leaves, grass, and other items they could forage. His mother told her son a warning tale, reminding him frequently that his older brother had been taken away by crazed cannibals at the age of four. This fact has not been confirmed, but it was repeated to the young Chikatilo every day, surrounded by the backdrop of poverty and war.

The Soviet entry into the Second World War meant that Chikatilo's father was drafted into the army. He was shortly wounded during a battle, captured, and taken prisoner. During the war period, Chikatilo would bear witness to many of the Nazi's atrocities committed during the occupation of Ukraine. These 'horrors' included fires, shootings, and bombings, during which he and the family would hide in the cellar. On some occasions, they were forced to hide in ditches. Once, the family had to stand by as their hut went up in flames. With his father gone, Chikatilo and his mother shared a bed. This became an issue when Andrei, a chronic bed wetter, would incur his mother's wrath.

Two years before the end of the war, with his father still in a prisoner camp, Chikatilo's mother became pregnant. She gave birth to a baby girl, Tatyana. Many have speculated that she was fathered by an occupying German soldier. Whether this was consensual or not is unknown.

During his school years, Andrei remembers occasionally fainting from the hunger brought about by the famine. He became the target for bullies, and his small stature made him an easy target for the larger and healthier children. At this point, Chikatilo began to develop a love of reading and discovered an ability to memorize large amounts of data. Being able to recall these large chunks of information boosted his self-worth and helped him to avoid problems during class, where poor eyesight often left him unable to read the blackboard. He received praise from his teachers, who remember him as an excellent student.

Chikatilo combined this status as an excellent student with his position as a model communist. At just fourteen, he took over the position of editor at his school's paper, becoming chairman of the school's communist committee just a couple of years later. A voracious reader of ideological literature, he helped to organize marches in the streets and became the single member of his collective farm to finish his studies.

As he entered into puberty, Chikatilo found that he was a sufferer of chronic impotence. For an already socially awkward teenager, this worsened his problems. He would remain a shy and isolated boy throughout his teen years. He applied to university, and despite excellent scores, was not awarded a place. Chikatilo himself thought his father's less than perfect war record – and the fact he had been branded a traitor - might be a blight upon his own reputation. Unknown to Chikatilo, however, the rejection was simply a case of other students achieving higher scores. Rather than attempting to apply to another school, Andrei turned to work. He began to learn a trade as a communications technician in Kursk and even began dating a local girl. Though he attempted to have sex with his girlfriend, his medical conditions prevented the relationship from being consummated. The couple split after a year and a half.

Next, Andrei would complete his compulsory military service. Just before the three years ended, he joined the local communist party. Once discharged from the military (with an excellent record), he returned to his parents' home. Again, he began dating a local girl and again the relationship fell apart for familiar reasons. When the girl asked her friends for advice, many of Chikatilo's peers discovered his medical condition. Speaking about this period, he recalls, "I was so ashamed. I tried to hang myself." His family caught him while he was trying to hang himself and saved Andrei's life. He ran away in shame. Up until this point in his life, Chikatilo had remained a tragic figure. This would all change in the coming years.

His Crimes

Chikatilo's first murder was committed just a few days before Christmas in 1978. Lena Zakotnova was just nine years old when she was tempted into a disused shed. Here, Chikatilo attempted to rape her. As she struggled, he lashed out with a knife. During the act and the struggle, Chikatilo ejaculated. This relationship between extreme violence and sexual pleasure would link many of his later crimes. Despite witnesses claiming to have seen Chikatilo with the girl before her disappearance, he was able to secure an iron clad alibi. Police left him alone. Instead, they arrested another man with a criminal record of rape and violence. After a typically brutal police interrogation, this man confessed to the crime and was executed. Perhaps scared of the close call, Chikatilo went quiet for three years.

After earning a reputation of untrustworthiness around children, Chikatilo found it was very difficult to acquire a teaching position. Instead, he moved to Rostov and worked as a clerk. It was the travel involved in this position which would provide him with a huge amount of access to his potential victims. His next victim was a seventeen-year-old girl named Larisa. She was choked, stabbed, and had dirt and leaves shoved down her throat. The ease of this murder and the sexual pleasure it brought him encouraged Chikatilo to focus his attentions on this demographic: teenagers who had run away from their homes. He would meet them at stations and act in a friendly manner. After luring them to an isolated spot (typically a forest), he would attack. His knife became a substitute for his penis. On occasions, he even went as far as to eat the genitalia of his victims or would take small body parts as trophies.

Detectives who reviewed the cases found that Chikatilo murders usually followed a pattern. They would involve a great deal of savage attacks to the eyes, slashing at and removing the eyes from their sockets. During this period, the very concept of a serial killer was not known in Ukraine or, indeed, the rest of the Soviet Union. On those occasions where there were rumors of a mass-murderer of some type, state media would clamp down on the news and forbid it from being broadcast or published. However, body counts are difficult to ignore, and the rising number of deaths at the hand of Chikatilo were variously attributed to werewolves or spy plots by the locals. Even without the media, the news of the deaths was enough to cause fear and worry among the public.

Noticing that there might be an issue in the area, the local police set a special task force to deal with Chikatilo. They employed a forensic analyst by the name of Victor Burakov to lead the investigation. Primarily, they looked at known sex offenders and those with known mental health concerns. While interviewing the various suspects, the brutality of their interrogation methods turned up several false confessions. Burakov was skeptical. At this point, the true extent of Chikatilo's killing was unknown, and not all of the bodies had been uncovered. Each time a corpse was found, however, it added to the mounting evidence. Soon, they had discerned the killer's blood type (AB) and collected grey hairs and semen samples from the scenes of the crimes. Throughout 1984, an additional fifteen victims were discovered. Police efforts increased accordingly.

A short while later, Chikatilo was arrested at a bus station. The reason given was his suspicious behavior, rather than any connection to the murders. He was imprisoned for three months due to several outstanding charges, but the testing of his blood returned no positive matches. Due to a medical abnormality, Chikatilo belonged to a very specific group of individuals for whom blood testing is sometimes not effective in crime detection. After three months, he walked free.

After being released, Chikatilo took a job as a travelling buyer for a train company buyer. Though based in Novocherkassk, the frequent travel allowed him to maintain a low profile. Despite this, he is known to have murdered a pair of women in the summer of 1985, each in a separate incident.
The lead investigator was beginning to become frustrated at the lack of developments in the case.

To accelerate his efforts, he drafted a well-known psychiatrist, Alexandr Bukhanovsky. Bukhanovsky was able to construct a profile of the serial killer which differed to the one already in use. He estimated the age at being much older than previously thought, around fifty or younger. The psychiatrist also described the "necro-sadism" of the killer, suspecting the unknown criminal gained a sexual gratification from the murders.

As well as this, Burakov elected to interview a captured serial killer in order to get an insight into the specific mindset. Anatoly Slivko was already in custody after committing many murders, and Burakov spent time in his company. During this time, however, the murders ceased. Police were under the suspicion that the serial killer had either stopped, had been incarcerated, or had died. The trail, once again, went cold.

That was until the early months of 1988, when Chikatilo returned to his task. When he started to return to his previous style – snatching victims from public transport areas – he noticed that the police had placed these areas under surveillance. He spent two years killing as many as nineteen people, the majority of whom were young boys. The police did note that their target was becoming increasingly willing to take risks, with many killings happening in public places.

Following the political events of Glasnost, the Gorbachev-led government began to place larger amounts of pressure on the police to catch their man. The killer was becoming more notorious by the day. Police patrols increased. Burakov believed that with the right manpower, he could flush out the killer.

He was nearly right. Several times, Chikatilo only narrowly escaped detection. However, his suspicious behavior was noted by a policeman on November 6, 1990. Chikatilo has just killed the woman who would be his final victim, Sveta Korostik. The policeman, noticing the odd behavior of the man, took Chikatilo's details. Due to his previous crimes, he was placed under surveillance, and men were tasked with knowing his whereabouts at all times.

The sentence

The capture of Andrei Chikatilo was less dramatic than might be expected. Following another case of suspicious behavior, he was hauled into the police station on November 20, 1990. Though police had their suspicions of his activities, he refused to confess to any murder. Stumped, Burakov decided to allow the police psychiatrist to interview Chikatilo. Bukhanovski had constructed the original profile which was becoming more apparently accurate by the minute. Entering the cell, Bukhanovski began talking to Chikatilo under the presence of wishing to learn more about the mind of a serial killer, rather than simply attributing guilt.

This approach flattered Chikatilo. With the doctor, he was more than happy to discuss not only his roles in the killings, but the murders themselves. In all, he claimed, Chikatilo had killed fifty-six people. At the time, police estimates were only attributing him with thirty-six. Later, Chikatilo would lead police to a number of the bodies.

After confessing his guilt and talking to the police and the medical staff, Chikatilo was declared legally sane and thus suitable to stand trial. The court date was set for April 14, 1992. As a special dispensation, Chikatilo was placed inside an iron cage in the court room, designed to separate the serial killer from the families of the people he had murdered.

The press, given new freedoms under the political regime, were keen to jump on the story of the man they described as "the Maniac" and "The Butcher of Rostov." Chikatilo's behavior reflected this interest, ranging from the mundane and the boring to the unpredictable and the manic. At points, Chikatilo stood in his iron cage and sang in a gibberish language. At one point, he supposedly pulled down his trousers and showed the entire court his genitals.

The court was less than sympathetic to the point of bias. Chikatilo's lawyer would often be overruled. It soon became apparent that the judge presiding over the case had already decided on the guilt of the accused. The trail lasted months, all the way until the end of August. Even despite the judge's predilections, the verdict was not delivered until two months later. Chikatilo was found guilty of fifty-two murders, one short of the fifty-three of which he had been accused. Each one carried the death penalty.

Chikatilo appealed the decision, claiming that the psychiatric evaluation was incorrect and that he was not sane enough to stand trial. He was unsuccessful. Sixteen months later, the court carried out its punishment. Chikatilo received a single shot to the back of his head. The date was February 14, 1994.

Chikatilo's appeal centered on the claim that the psychiatric evaluation that had found him fit to stand trial was biased, but this process was unsuccessful. The case was one of the first of its type in Russia and Ukraine. In Andrei Chikatilo, a country with a violent and bloodied past was given its first high profile serial killer.

A man who earned the trust of tourists and killed them for their money

Charles Sobhraj

Also known as the Splitting Killer

The setting

While many serial killers strike out at unassuming victims under the cover of darkness and mystery, some reach out from under the cover of friendship. Chales Sobhraj was a killer who earned the trust of travelers and preyed on a belief in the kindness of strangers. He was born in Saigon, the son of a Vietnamese mother and an Indian father who were not married. His father would later leave the family to fend for themselves. After his mother met a new boyfriend, Sobhraj was adopted by the French Army lieutenant with whom his mother had fallen in love. After the couple had children of their own, Charles would find his parental affections sidelined. The family moved back and forth between France and South East Asia, and Charles began to develop an interest in petty and minor crimes.

This interest would result in a first jail sentence after being caught committing burglary in 1963. He served his time in a Parisian jail, using his charm to convince the guards to permit him special privileges. Unlike other prisoners, he was allowed to keep books in his cell. One man who volunteered at the prison was Felix d'Escogne, a wealthy individual with whom Sobhraj struck up a friendship. After being released, he would move in with Felix, splitting his interests between the criminal underworld and the bourgeoisie Parisian upper classes. Using a series of thefts and scams, he built up a small fortune of his own. It was during this time he met Chantal Compagnon, the daughter of a conservative family. On the day he asked for her hand in marriage, Sobhraj was arrested for being the driver of a stolen vehicle. He served eight months in jail. The couple married when he was once again a free man.

Together, they travelled to French controlled areas of Asia to avoid the attentions of the law. They would use falsified documents and would rob tourists who they began to befriend. Finally, in 1970, they arrived in Mumbai with their daughter, Usha. Sobhraj turned back to a life of crime. He organized a vehicle stealing operation, smuggling the cars in and out of the country.

Rather than spending his profits on his family, he developed an addiction to gambling.

After attempting to rob a jewelry store in 1970, Sobhraj was arrested. He escaped by enlisting his wife's help in feigning an illness. Despite getting free, they were soon recaptured, and Sobhraj was forced to borrow money from his father to pay his bail. The family took flight and journeyed to Kabul.

Here, they began their business of robbing visitors to what became known as "the hippie trail." They befriended foreigners, offered guidance, and then took their belongings. He was once again arrested and used the same illness trick to escape. This time, when fleeing to Iran, Sobhraj did not bring his family. Chantal was beginning to have doubts about their life style, and she returned to France with their daughter. Over the next two years, Sobhraj attempted to evade the law. With nearly a dozen stolen passports, he moved through Eastern Europe and the Middle East. He connected with his younger brother, Andre when he reached Instanbul, when the two quickly struck up a criminal relationship. Andre was captured in Greece. Charles escaped but was forced to leave his brother behind to serve an eighteen-year sentence.

His Crimes

The real crimes would begin now, as Sobhraj began to pose as either a drug dealer or a gem expert, working his magic on tourists as they travelled across Asia. Once ingratiated, he would rob his new friends and run. During this time, he began to build up a cadre of devoted followers, people who trusted Sobhraj completely and were content to do his bidding.

He would often arrange for difficult situations for travelers to enter into. Missing passports was a familiar scheme, with tourists scared of how they might recover their lost documents. In reality, they had already been stolen, but Sobhraj would befriend and help the victims before robbing them of even more money. He might suggest that a tourist had contracted dysentery when, in fact, they had been poisoned at his hand. A young Indian man named Ajay Chowdhury would become the second in command of Sobhraj's expanding criminal crew.

The first murders were committed in 1975. Later police investigations revealed the first victims to be members of the crew who threatened to reveal Sobhraj's crimes to the authorities. The girl – Teresa Knowlton from Seattle – was discovered, her body floating in a pool near the

Thai coast. She had been drowned. First thought to be an accident, a later autopsy revealed the true nature of her death months later. The next victim was Vitalli Hakim, whose burned body was found near the gang's hiding place in Pattaya.

One example of the gang's murderous modus operandi was the case of Henk Bintanja and Cornelia Hemker, a betrothed Dutch couple in their late twenties. They met Sobhraj in Hong Kong and were convinced to travel with him to Thailand. There, they were poisoned and nursed back to health by the crew. This act gained their trust, with everyone telling them they had contracted an illness. Worried about attracting attention, the couple were strangled, their bodies burned and dumped near the gang's hideout. The gang then took the pair's passports and used them to travel to Nepal.

This process continued, meeting tourists, befriending them, killing them, and stealing their wealth and travelling documents. Once the act of murder had been committed, Sobhraj and his gang would move to the next country before the bodies could be identified. The gang followed Sobhraj across countries and continents, including visits to Calcutta, Bangkok, and Nepal. Difficulties in tracking the fake names and a lack of collusion between police meant the scope of their actions was not realized. In the West, countries such as the Netherlands and France began to investigate reports of teenagers disappearing during their travels. There were even instances of governments covering up the murders, with countries such as Thailand fearing that the reveal of the murders would lead to a fall in the tourism industry.

Leading the investigation in Holland was a diplomat named Herman Knippenberg. He had become aware of Sobhraj's criminal activities. It is reported that he may even have met the man, though Sobhraj's name was still unknown at this point. Using the evidence he gathered with the help of a neighbor, Knippenberg was granted a search warrant for Sobhraj's apartment. Inside, he found stolen documents and passports, in addition to poisons and medical equipment.

Meanwhile, Sobhraj's gang of three was travelling through Malaysia. At this point, Chowdury went missing, with witnesses recalling him giving Sobhraj a large number of jewels. Now working with just one partner, Sobhraj travelled to Geneva and posed as a gem salesman. Though his death had been unconfirmed, no trace of Chowdury was ever been substantiated. With the proceeds from this sale, Sobhraj began to recruit members for his gang. During this time, their actions brought about the death of Luc Solomon, a Frenchman the gang poisoned. Designed to incapacitate him and build trust, the poison instead took his life.

Sobhraj was captured in New Delhi in 1976. Having convinced a group of French students to let him be their tour guide, he provided them with what he described as anti-dysentery tablets. When the poison began to act quicker than anticipated, several of the students fell unconscious. Realizing what was happening, those still awake attacked Sobhraj and detained him. They handed him over to the authorities with a description of his crimes. Police also began to question the members of his gang. While Sobhraj held out, his newly recruited accomplices quickly cracked. They confessed to the murders. Sobhraj was charged and sent to prison in Tihar as he awaited the beginning of his trial.

The sentence

Inside the jail, conditions were so tough as to drive two of the gang into attempting suicide. They would remain in this jail for two years as the trial was put together. Unlike his fellow criminals, however, Sobhraj had been in possession of many gems when entering the jail. Using these, he bought and bartered for special privileges, turning his incarceration into a more pleasant experience.

When the trial started, Sobhraj exhibited his flair for showmanship. Attracting media attention, he would fire and hire lawyers frequently, even recruiting his newly released brother Andre as part of the legal team. He starved himself, telling people he was hunger striking. Despite this, he was sentenced to jail for a period of twelve years. With many predicting the death penalty, it was thought Sobhraj had gotten off lightly.

Inside the jail, Sobhraj began to exert his influence and bribed many of the guards. Leading a "life of luxury," his television and gourmet meals were a result of a friendship with both guards and prisoners. He began to spread his fame worldwide, encouraging Western authors and journalists to write about his life. He discussed his murders freely, describing events without ever actually admitting to his own involvement. His motives, he began to suggest, were to avenge the history of Western imperialism in Asia.

Despite his incarceration in India, Sobhraj was still a wanted man. An arrest warrant in Thailand would mean being tried for crimes punishable by death. On the tenth anniversary of his time in jail, he used his influence to throw a huge party for the guards and the prisoners alike. Here, he poisoned all in attendance and simply walked out of the jail. He was arrested in Goa while eating at a restaurant and was sentenced to a further ten years. This had been his plan all the long. By the time he was finally released again, the warrant for his arrest had expired, witnesses had disappeared, and evidence had been lost. With no outstanding criminal charges, he was allowed to return to France.

Returning to Paris, Sobhraj began to revel in his own notoriety. He recruited a publicity agent to spread his fame and charged the press for access to his story. It is thought that he accrued close to fifteen million dollars in this manner by selling the rights to a film based on his story.

In 2003, he returned to Nepal for unknown reasons. Here, he was captured and thrown in jail. Quickly, Sobhraj moved to have the case squashed and complained about his lack of a fair trial. In France, his estranged wife Chantal was said to be submitting a case to the European Court of Human Rights, due to the fact that the French government refused to provide assistance. In 2005, his conviction was deemed to be legitimate. After being at the center of three documentary films and four books, some have suggested that Charles Sobhraj was desperate for attention and returned to Nepal to increase interest in his own notoriety. He resides in jail to this day, found guilty of a number of murders. As he still protests his innocence, we may never know the true extent of his prolific killing spree.

The man whose hammer and knife created a campaign of terror

Peter Sutcliffe

Also known as the Yorkshire Ripper

The setting

As we have discussed previously in this book, many experts trace the modern concept of the serial killer back to the crimes of the man known as Jack the Ripper in Victorian England. As one of the lasting legacies of these crimes, the suffix "ripper" has been used to describe a number of modern killers. One of the most infamous is Peter Sutcliffe, the man who came to be known in the press as the Yorkshire Ripper.

Sutcliffe – as his alias suggests – was a native of the north English town of Yorkshire. He came from a working class background, born into a family who were strongly linked to the Catholic faith. As a noted loner and isolated figure during his childhood, he left school at the age of fifteen without feeling the need to pursue his education. In the working world, he began to search for a job, taking on a number of menial positions at this time. One of the most memorable was his time as a gravedigger in the 1960s. He worked in the packing department of a television company, and then, when asked to become a travelling salesman for the same company, he left.

After this, he took time off from his temporary night job to earn his truck driving license. His first position in this industry – delivering tires for a local company – resulted in him being dismissed for suspected theft. He variously held a number of positions as a truck driver throughout the 1970s, during which time it is suspected he began soliciting prostitutes. One of the formative experiences attributed to him by experts is the possible losing of a large amount of money to one such sex worker.

In 1974, he married his girlfriend, Sonia Szurma. They had met seven years previously and, after several attempts to conceive a child, they discovered that Sonia was unable to become a mother. Instead, she resumed her training to become a teacher and entered into an affair with an ice cream seller. Sutcliffe remained unaware. The two bought a house using Sonia's earnings as a teacher. They would still be living in this home when Sutcliffe was later arrested.

Doctors and experts who examined Sutcliffe's early life have stated that they were unable to find anything distinctly abnormal during his childhood. However, his early adulthood – and in particular his time working digging graves – had an adverse effect on his personality. During this time, he began to build a reputations as a dark and macabre person, noted for his twisted humor. He is also noted for his voyeuristic attitudes and his repeated spying on prostitutes and various sex workers from a distance.

His Crimes

It is widely regarded that Sutcliffe's history as a serial killer began in 1969. His first act was to assault an older prostitute. Searching for the money he believed he had been scammed out of, he travelled with a friend to search for the woman. During his search, he vanished up a road, out of sight of his friend. Upon his return, he was noticeably out of breath and instructed his friend to drive away quickly. According to Sutcliffe, he followed the woman into a garage and hit her over the head with a rock stowed inside a sock. In his own words, the force of the blow was enough to tear the toe of the sock, sending the stone flying across the room. The assaulted woman noted the license plate of the vehicle in which they escaped and called the police. To the police, Sutcliffe said he had used his hand to hit the woman. The woman, according to the police, was unwilling to press further charges and wanted nothing more to do with the incident. The police left Sutcliffe alone.

The second violent incident came several years later, in the summer of 1975. Anna Rogulskyj was walking by herself when attacked. This was the first instance of Sutcliffe using the weapon he would come to be associated with: a ball-peen hammer. As well as hitting her over the head, Sutcliffe used a knife to slash open her stomach. The attack was interrupted by a neighbor, and Rogulskyj survived. A medical procedure managed to save her life, but she was left traumatized by the attack.

The Yorkshire Ripper's next victim was Olive Smelt. Sutcliffe attacked in the same manner, using the combination of a hammer and a knife to take down his victim from behind. Once again, Sutcliffe was interrupted, and Smelt was left alive but traumatized. The same month, fourteen-year-old Tracy Browne was attacked, again with the hammer. After being disturbed during the attack by the lights of a passing car, Sutcliffe left Browne where she lay. She would survive but would need brain surgery.

The first woman Sutcliffe killed was Wilma McCann. A mother of four, Wilma died on October 30. She was struck twice over the head before being slashed with the knife fifteen times. Investigators would find traces of semen on her clothes. Her death would alert the police to the seriousness of the crimes being committed.

It would be four months before Sutcliffe's next murder. Emily Jackson was stabbed fifty-one times by Sutcliffe. Having fallen on dire financial times, Jackson had begun to solicit sexual clients using a family-owned van. Once Sutcliffe had hit her over the head with his hammer, he sharpened a screwdriver to a point. He drove it into her neck, her abdomen, and her chest. Finally, he stomped on Jackson's thigh and left behind the imprint of his boot.

The third killing of 1976 would be Marcella Claxton, who was attacked while walking home from a party on May 9. Needing to urinate, she left her car on the side of the road. Sutcliffe came from behind and hit her with his hammer. Although she was left wounded on the side of the road, Claxton survived. She would be one of the witnesses who would testify at Sutcliffe's trial.

The following February, a prostitute named Irene Richardson was attacked in Roundhay Park. Another victim who was hit over the head with the hammer, Richardson would be one of the bodies with whom Sutcliffe interfered following her death. He used his knife to mutilate her corpse but again left behind a clue for investigators. The tire marks of his vehicle were readily identifiable at the scene of the crime.

The next murder was Patricia Atkinson. On April 23, she was killed in her flat, and once again, Sutcliffe left behind a print of his boot, this time on Atkinson's bed sheets. Jayne MacDonald, just sixteen at the time of the attack, was killed two months later. The fact that she was not a sex worker opened the public's eyes to the potential threat the Yorkshire Ripper posed to all women, regardless of their profession.

Maureen Long was attacked in July but survived. Sutcliffe attempted to murder Long but was interrupted and forced to flee. Witnesses described what they saw to the police but incorrectly identified the car Sutcliffe was driving. By this point, over three hundred policemen had been drafted into the investigation. Though thousands of car registrations were checked, but nothing was found since the investigations were built on incorrect accounts. On October 1, Jean Jordan was killed by Sutcliffe, but her body was not found for ten days. It appeared that the body had been moved several days after the murder, as Sutcliffe had realized a bank note he had passed to the victim would be traceable. When arriving back at the body, Sutcliffe could not find the note and instead mutilated the corpse and moved it to another location.

Jordan's body would be discovered the morning after it had been moved. She had been hidden near an allotment garden and was found by a dairy worker tending to his own plants. The traceable note was stashed away in a hidden compartment of Jordan's handbag, and its discovery would play a key role in tracking down the killer. Thanks to the particular note, police were able to trace the location to a specific branch. Police analysis of bank operations allowed them to narrow their field of inquiry to eight thousand employees who could have received it in their wage packet. They followed this up by interviewing thousands of employers who might have included the note in an employee's pay packet. Over three months, the police interviewed five thousand men, including Sutcliffe. During his interview, the alibi Sutcliffe provided was deemed to be credible. The party he had attended was one he later left in order to commit the crimes, but those at the party were able to confirm his attendance. This meant the vital clue found by investigators had led nowhere.

The final attack of 1977 was Marilyn Moore, a sex worker from Leeds. She lived and was able to provide the police with a description of the man who attacked her. As well as this, tire imprints from the crime scene matched those found at an earlier attack.

In 1978, Sutcliffe killed three women. His final attack of the year came in May, after which it was almost a year before he struck again. During this time, Sutcliffe was dealing with the death of his mother. His next victim was Josephine Whitaker, who was attacked on April 4, 1979. She was a clerk for a building society and had been walking home from work. The police had become distracted by a recording sent to their headquarters purporting to be by the Ripper. Based on the accent, investigators tracked their suspect down to a specific area of Sunderland. The messages were, however, a hoax. John Humble would later be convicted for attempting to pervert the course of justice.

Sutcliffe's next victim was Barbara Leach, a local student. She was the sixteenth victim. Her body was placed beneath a pile of bricks near her university. At this point – even in spite of the red herring voice messages – Sutcliffe was interviewed by police on two more occasions. This count would eventually reach nine, and even though he had been placed on a shortlist of three hundred suspects, he was not among the highest ranking in police thoughts.

In April of 1980, Peter Sutcliffe was caught driving under the influence of alcohol. While he awaited trial for this crime, two more women were killed. Sutcliffe also attacked three further women who managed to survive. On November 25, a known associate of Sutcliffe named Trevor Birdsall reported his friend as a possible suspect. This was added to a pile of ever mounting paperwork.

The sentence

Sutcliffe was caught on January 2, 1981. Stopped by police, he was in the company of a prostitute named Olivia Reivers. The police checked the vehicle and found it to be fitted with false license plates. Sutcliffe was arrested. Police questioned him in connection with the Ripper murders and noted his likeness to physical descriptions of the killer. The next day, they discovered a hammer, a knife, and a rope that had been stashed in the car during his arrest. A second knife had been hidden in the cistern of a police toilet during his time in custody. They wrote a search warrant for his home and began to question his wife.

Police inspected Sutcliffe's clothes and found him to be wearing a specially fitted pullover beneath his trousers, the neck hole designed to provide access to his genitals during an attack. Padding around his knees had been added and would allow him to crouch down over his victims. This information and the sexual implications it contained were not revealed to the public until 2003. Police interrogated Sutcliffe for forty-eight hours until, quite suddenly, he confessed to being the Yorkshire Ripper. Once this admission was made, he proceeded to describe in detail many of his attacks. After several weeks, he declared God had told him to commit the murders. Of all the accounts, only the story of Jayne MacDonald (his youngest victim) brought forth an emotional response.

At trial, Sutcliffe entered a not guilty to thirteen murder charges. He instead asked for a charge of manslaughter based on reasons of insanity, referencing the will of God in his attacks. He suggested that he had begun to hear voices while digging graves, voices that had ordered him to murder sex workers. Of all the graves, it was the grave of Bronisław Zapolski that Sutcliffe suggested made the demands. He also pleaded guilty to the attempted murder of seven women. His diminished responsibility plea was rejected, and the trial lasted two weeks. Peter Sutcliffe was found guilty of thirteen murders and sentenced to life in jail. He remains in prison to this day. During his incarceration, he has been at the center of four different attempts on his life, losing an eye during one attack. Politicians have constantly reiterated that it is unlikely he will ever be viable for parole.

Conclusion

As you can tell from the number and variety of the cases we have examined, the profile of a serial killer is never an open and shut case. With so many motivations and so many deviations from the conventional morality we have come to expect in society, trying to predict or explain all of the actions of these individuals would be difficult if not impossible.

Due to the extreme nature of the crimes of serial killers, interest in their stories will always be high. Acting as both a morality tale and a warning to others, the prospect of an individual succumbing to the temptation to kill, mutilate, and destroy will always be something that fascinates many people. With some craving an explanation, others simply need to know that many of history's most evil men and women have been properly caught, tried, and punished.

However, with so many different serial killers existing both now and in the past, there will never be an end to the stories we tell.

Excerpts from Jack Smith's Book By Person or Persons...Unknown

Prologue

French sociologist Emil Durkheim once said that the violent criminal contributes to the well-being of society by promoting a sense of solidarity among those of us who obey the law. In other words, those who might not normally relate to one another are united in condemnation of the miscreant. In his 1926 essay *The Penalty of Death*, H. L. Mencken added that punishing said criminal restores the community's equilibrium:

> Every law-abiding citizen feels menaced and frustrated until the criminals have been struck down – until the communal capacity to get even with them, and more than even, has been dramatically demonstrated. Here, manifestly, the business of deterring others is no more than an afterthought. The main thing is to destroy the concrete scoundrels whose act has alarmed everyone, and thus made everyone unhappy. Until they are brought to book

that unhappiness continues; when the law has been executed upon them there is a sigh of relief. In other words, there is catharsis.

What if the criminal or criminals are never punished? Or even conclusively identified?

When this happens, there is a vacuum that continually demands to be filled, even decades after the crime was committed. This is why unsolved crimes – in this instance, murders – are rarely forgotten entirely.

This volume examines three cases of unsolved murders that continue to fascinate and horrify us:

- **The Murder of Margaret Blake:** On April 23, 1816, Margaret Blake was found in her decrepit cellar apartment, dead from a stab wound. Three people – her husband and two boarders – were present when it happened, but none of them were declared guilty. Modern forensic investigative techniques have been applied to this 200-year-old murder and have resulted in what may be the final solution.

- **The Mad Axeman of New Orleans:** From 1918-1919, a series of mysterious and gruesome axe murders terrified the Crescent City. The majority of the victims were Italians, but citizens of all backgrounds worried that their skulls would be caved in while they slept. The killer or killers were never caught, but recent research suggests a seminal form of organized crime directed the assaults.

- **The Grimes Murders of 1956:** A few days before New Year's Eve, 1957, 15-year-old Barbara Grimes and her 13-year-old sister Patricia left their Chicago home to see their idol, Elvis Presley's newest film. Weeks later, their naked bodies were found southwest of the city. Doctors could not pinpoint a primary cause of death and the murders remain unsolved.

These crimes are only a mere sample of the world's best-known unsolved murders. Despite advancements in forensic science and investigative techniques, more cases are added to this list every year. Detectives today have better training and more resources than their predecessors who investigated the Jack the Ripper murders of 1888, yet the killer or killers of JonBenet Ramsey remain free.

Perhaps one day, mandatory DNA samples will reduce the number of cases that go unsolved, but given the human rights question this entails, it likely won't happen. When a murder defies immediate solution, the only thing that can be done is keep the case – and the cause – alive until more evidence comes to light.

The Murder of Margaret Blake

The murder of Margaret Blake on April 23, 1816, is a case so cold it's positively freezing. Almost 200 years have passed since an unknown party stabbed her in the chest in a decrepit cellar apartment on Anthony Street in New York. The question of who did it remains one of antebellum New York City's biggest mysteries.

Was it her husband? Or one of the two women who boarded with the Blakes?

Or was it someone else entirely? Someone who thrust a knife between her ribs when neither her husband nor the female boarders were home, and then disappeared, never to have their name associated with the case?

On February 14, 1915, the *New York Times* referred to the murder in a feature entitled *Mysteries That Have Defied Solution.*

"Murder, we are told, will out. Yet nearly 100 years have passed since Margaret Blake was stabbed to the heart as she lay by her husband's side in a humble New York tenement....

After reviewing the suspect list and wondering which one could have wielded the knife, the writer added, "*Twelve good men and true could not decide on a certain July day in the year 1816, nor has time solved the mystery.*"[1]

The killer's name remains unknown nearly two centuries later. But thanks to a recent review of Margaret Blake's autopsy report by a UK pathologist, the circumstances of her death become much clearer.

******

Anthony Street was one of the main thoroughfares in the Five Points, a squalid region of Manhattan that was notorious for violence, vice, and poverty. Taking its name from a five-point intersection created by Anthony, Orange, and Cross Streets, it was a breeding ground for disease and crime. People crammed like sardines into filthy apartments and boarding houses, with the respectable poor breathing the same air as gangsters and petty criminals. The area had once been occupied by artisans, but in 1816 the residents were almost exclusively black or Irish.

---

[1] *New York Times*, February 14, 1915

The Five Points intersection in 1859 (Library of Congress)

Sometime between 8:00 and 9:00 p.m. on April 23, Paterick Blake came home from his laboring job. He was exhausted, hungry, and in a garrulous mood. When he opened the door to the one-room cellar apartment, he found his wife, Margaret, lying in bed and in no condition to cook supper. He assumed she was drunk and frowned. He and Margaret had often argued over her drinking, sometimes violently.

Catherine M'Gee, one of two women who boarded with Paterick and Margaret Blake, later testified at the murder trial:

All that day I had been away, and returned at about five o'clock in the afternoon, and found the deceased in bed.... About eight or nine o'clock in the evening, the prisoner (Blake), *who is a laborer, returned from his work, and deceased was still in bed. He went to the bed and said something to her, and she answered, but what I cannot say. I had spoken to deceased in the afternoon, and asked her to get up, to which she answered, "Let me alone," and I thought she was drunk. After the prisoner returned, I went to getting supper.*[2]

Mrs. Blake was huddled on the mattress, blankets around her chin and face pale. She replied when spoken to, but otherwise remained silent when Catherine M'Gee and the other boarder, Jane M'Fall, prepared a simple but hearty meal of fish and potatoes.

Once the food was ready, the table was pulled up to the Blakes' bed. Paterick Blake ate while sitting on the edge of the mattress and offered a plate to his wife, but she mumbled something about not being hungry.

---

[2] Lawson, J. (1972). *American state trials: A collection of the important and interesting criminal trials which have taken place in the United States, from the beginning of our government to 1920 : With notes and annotations.* Wilmington, Del.: Scholarly Resources, p.735

At around 10:00 p.m., the small household prepared for bed. Still believing that Margaret was drunk, Catherine M'Gee went to bind a handkerchief around her head. (Head-binding was a contemporary remedy for easing the headache pain of a hangover.) As she did so, she noticed a small amount of blood on the back of Margaret's hand. (She later said that the amount "might have proceeded from a scratch".)

Blake, who was sitting at the foot of the bed, snapped at her to leave his wife alone. When Mrs. McGee commented on the small blood smear, he growled that it was none of her business. Soon afterward, he got into bed. The two boarders had a short, sentimental conversion about Ireland, with Margaret occasionally commenting. Then all was quiet until 4:00 a.m., when Catherine M'Gee woke up to find an ashen-faced Blake standing at her bedside, holding a candle.

"I am afraid that Peggy (Margaret) is dead," he said. "She will not speak to me."

Catherine sat up. "That cannot be. She was well enough last night. Perhaps she is asleep – try to wake her up."

While she watched, Blake returned to his bed, seized his wife by the shoulders, and shook her, exclaiming her name over and over. But there was no response. He then lifted her slightly, causing the blankets to fall away and revealing blood all over the front of her nightgown.

Margaret Blake was obviously dead. Paterick laid her back down and moaned, “I am a poor man this morning!” Then he left the apartment and hurried through the chilly dawn to a small house occupied by his friends, the Hanleys. Already startled to be roused out of bed at such an early hour, the couple was doubly shocked to hear Paterick exclaim, “Peggy is dead!”

They followed him back to the Anthony Street dwelling, where the sight of the bloody corpse and bedstead filled them with horror. Catherine M’Gee and Jane M’Fall hovered nearby, blinking as if trying to awaken from a terrible nightmare.

The Hanleys stayed for over an hour, during which time Blake went out again and returned with his grown son. Then he left a third time, but not to escape or flee. He went to the office of John Bedient, Coroner for the City of New York, and reported Margaret’s death.

"Did she die in a fit?" Bedient asked after hearing the details. Blake replied that he had no idea and insisted that the coroner accompany him back to the tenement.

At the scene, Bedient carefully lifted the bedclothes from Margaret's body and observed a wound under her left breast. The blankets were searched for the presence of a discarded weapon, but nothing was found. Bedient later testified that Blake, who hovered over him, "appeared totally... insensible."

The coroner sent for surgeons to examine the wound. The medical men found that the weapon had passed between the cartilages of the fifth and sixth vertebrae. Seeing an old scar near the injury one of the surgeons, Dr. Alexander Stevens, asked Blake what had caused it. He answered that Margaret had once fallen on a knife she was holding.

After the surgeons concluded their examination, Bedient asked the coroner's jury, which had been hastily assembled on site, if they wanted to examine Blake. They did, so the now-widower took off his coat, his movements slow and mechanical. Bedient immediately spotted blood on his right inner arm and under his fingernails.

“How did that (blood) get there?” the coroner asked.

Blake, who still seemed to be in shock, responded that he didn’t know. He also said that the door had been bolted from the inside throughout the night and was still bolted when he opened it to go for the neighbors.

A policeman named Abner Curtis, who had been searching the apartment, found a bloody jackknife with a four-inch blade. When Blake confirmed that it was his but didn’t know where the blood came from, the dazed widower was taken into custody and held on a charge of murder.

Domestic violence was routine in the Five Points, and it rarely came to the attention of the authorities. Unless, of course, it ended in murder. Then the guilty party headed for the gallows, provided that their guilt could be proven. This fate appeared to be in store for Paterick Blake, who’d been covered in his wife’s blood when arrested and was known to have quarreled violently with her in the past.

The death of Margaret Blake appeared to be an open and shut case. Except that it wasn’t.

***

OTHER BOOKS FROM JACK SMITH

Folkloric Fae

A Folkloric Prequel Novella

Karenza Grant

L'Ours

A L'OURS BOOKS ebook

Ebook first published in 2023 by L'Ours Books

Cover: Deranged Doctor Design

Copyediting: Toby Selwyn

ISBN (print) 978-1-915737-08-3

Also available in ebook

www.karenzagrant.com

To Dodo

Folkloric Fae

A few months before Folkloric...

Chapter 1

I should have been working. I should have been clearing tables or serving the best patisserie in the South of France. But instead, I was listening to Shroom-Jean.

Or rather, I wasn't listening to the guy as he was staring vacantly into the blazing hearth at our side. For the fifth time since I'd started the interview, he was on another planet.

My phone sat on the table between us, recording the non-existent conversation. I glanced at the time on the screen. Two minutes longer than I'd said I'd be. A sizeable queue had built at the counter, and Alice was frazzled as she rushed to take orders. I really needed to finish this up and help her out.

"Oh, yeah... where was I...?" He scratched his head, ruffling straight grey hair that fell to his chest. As he lowered his hand, he knocked his glasses askew. "Sorry, Camille. I remember what I was going to say." Grinning,

he straightened his glasses. "Back then, in my grandfather's day, he had to walk three miles to school no matter the weather. And he was lucky. My great-uncle had to walk ten miles."

I tapped my fingers on the table. Yes, Jean had managed to zone back into reality, but he'd gone off track again, and if I didn't do something, we'd be here all day. "Uh, Jean. You were telling me about your grandmother's account of the goblin, and how it used to ruin her baking sessions."

If I could just get to the end of his story, it wouldn't feel like wasted effort. The local folklore society was recording fairy accounts for prosperity. As the older generations passed away, stories were at risk of being lost. I'd already collected three others—and they hadn't been easy to get. The old tales were mostly recollections of the grandparents or great-grandparents of the elderly, and I'd had to sit through more than my fair share of detailed family histories along the way. But the folklore fascinated me, not to mention my contribution meant I was beginning to make a name for myself in the local research community, and that wasn't easy, unqualified as I was.

Jean paused, his gentle gaze filming over again. "I was telling you about the goblin, was I? Oh yes... the goblin." He took a sip of his cappuccino and scraped up the crumbs of the three Danish pastries I'd bought him as a thank you for the interview. But by the look of his scrawny arms and his concave middle that hid under the peace symbol on his

faded pink T-shirt, he needed feeding up more regularly. "Well, it wasn't so much the baking that the little critter disrupted, Granny used to say..." He trailed off again and searched the room as though he'd left his focus on the bread counter, or with one of the customers sheltering espressos in comfy armchairs. Finally he gazed into the fire again, its blaze fierce against the end-of-January snow outside.

I scraped my hands through my hair, frustration clenching my fingers. No doubt I was mussing the dark locks I'd pinned into a ponytail, but I didn't really care. I just needed one minute... one short minute of Jean staying firmly in the here and now.

A horn blared. I turned to the noise, catching my harsh and rather exasperated reflection in the window. Just a truck on the N20. The traffic was busy—folks travelling from all parts of France to the ski resorts deep in the Pyrenees mountains. Tarascon, and particularly Pyrenee's café, made an ideal stop-off.

I followed the glimmering headlights as cars ploughed through the blizzard, the terrible visibility bringing an early dusk. Dark combinations of snow and twilight shifted and swirled in the glass. To my folklore-obsessed imagination, the storm formed leering goblins, prowling hell hounds and massive-jawed croquembouches—the nasty ogres Alice and I had been so scared of when we were little. I was sure I'd dreamt about them last night, but I couldn't grasp the memory. My thick, completely unrefreshing sleep had made me late for work again this morn-

ing. Honestly, I had folklore on the brain, and it wasn't healthy.

One of the croquembouche shapes shifted closer, distorting snow-covered cars in the parking area. Cold darkness crept in on the café, my skin prickling. I shuddered. But, come on. Was the thought of a childhood bogeyman actually scaring me?

"Ummm, Camille?" Jean said.

I jumped, my heart pounding. "Uh, sorry, Jean, I was miles away."

"Not to worry." He grinned back. "Lack of focus isn't something I suffer from, fortunately." He waggled his glasses. "I've got the attention of a hawk."

I was at a loss for words. Did he really not realise he spent most of the time out to lunch? But anyway, I was zoning out way harder.

"You know," Jean added, nodding to the window, "this time of year, winter either dies or it becomes stronger. It will start to ease, or it will be like this for a while longer."

I couldn't wait for the spring—for warmth and light—but we needed to get back on track. I released a steadying breath. "The baking and your grandmother..."

"Yes. It wasn't the actual baking in the oven the goblin messed with, it was the rising of the bread." He was on topic. I willed him to keep going, but still I could see unnerving shapes—a leering eye here, a set of ridiculously large jaws there. I blinked rapidly, attempting to clear my head. Talk about intrusive thoughts.

Jean pulled out a colourful bead necklace from his T-

shirt and twisted it. "When that little fella was around, no matter what Granny Berger did, she could not get the dough to rise. There would be faint cackles of laughter, and she knew it was the goblin. Eventually, Granny found that if she left it a small cup of milk on the hearth the night before baking, it would be sure to leave her in peace. And... that was it, really."

My shoulders fell. Jean had made it to the end. Admittedly, I'd had reservations about Shroom-Jean as a source. He'd earned his nickname for a reason. But his recollection was typical of the era, which gave it the mark of authenticity. If he'd tripped the whole thing, surely it would've been a lot more colourful.

I clicked off my phone. "Thank you, Jean. I appreciate it very much. It's a lovely story, and now it will be recorded for posterity. I have to say, I'm intrigued that folk used to believe goblins caused problems in their daily lives. I guess it was a way of explaining bad stuff happening."

Jean looked at me quizzically. "Yeah, there's that," he said. "But what's more likely? A trustworthy and respected woman making up something so strange, or a goblin actually existing." His eyes grew wide and expectant.

"Uh..." Of course, old Granny Berger probably had a cold draft on her dough, and she'd made up the creature to entertain her grandson when he was small. But, knowing Jean's outlook on the world, he'd go for the goblin existing. "I see your point," I replied in my best neutral voice.

He nodded, satisfied. "And that's not the only story. I've got a couple more, if you're interested?"

Was I interested? I was fascinated by the way people of old chose to shape the good, the bad and the ugly into the existence of fairies. And I'd gain extra points with the Folklore Society. "I'd love to, but I can't now. Any chance you'd be around the day after tomorrow? I'd do tomorrow, but we're going to be even shorter-staffed—"

"Jean, great to see you!" Inès called from across the café as she hobbled in our direction, a few bagged-up loaves in her arms, her steely curls restrained by a head-scarf. The gentle curves of her face that she'd passed on to Alice were a reflection of the warmth of the café. She'd put all her love into the creation of the place.

"Inès!" Jean rose to meet her and they exchanged kisses. "It's been a while. How are you?" Inès's face was flushed—there was usually a hint of pink in her complexion from working in the kitchen, but today she appeared almost maroon.

"Very well," she replied with a broad smile, her warm eyes creasing at the corners. "Here, I've baked too much fougasse. I couldn't get rid of some in your direction, could I?"

I knew for a fact Inès hadn't baked too much. She was very precise, and she'd been training up Guy today, focussing on maintaining quality whilst reducing waste. She'd noticed Jean's lean body too. There was little shepherding work for him in the winter when the flocks were in the lower pastures.

"Don't mind me, you two," I said, thinking of a hideous croquembouche as I rose. "I have to get back to work."

"Did you get what you needed?" Inès rubbed my arm in moral support, her lips pursing. She knew what Jean was like.

"I sure did." I pointed at Jean and raised my brow. "Same time day after tomorrow?"

"Gotcha," he replied, then tumbled into conversation with Inès.

I skirted the queue and headed behind the counter, then grabbed an apron and tied it on over my jeans and jumper. But as I did so, thoughts of dark creatures with foul leers and mirthless grins forced in on me once again, the images unnervingly clear. They felt like more than my folklore-addled brain or the fragments of a dream—they felt like an invasion.

Chapter 2

"Sorry I was so long," I said, taking over the bagging up of orders as Alice handled the till.

"No worries, hon." She shot me a grin. "Get your story?"

"Eventually."

Alice's eyes held their usual soft sparkle, though her choppy shoulder-length hair was more dishevelled than usual, contrasting her fifties top and slacks. "That will be ten euros," she said to the customer, then nodded to Inès and Jean, who were still in conversation. "My mother is killing me." She scowled as she took another order. "She just won't stop working. Her chronic fatigue is worse and she was in agony again yesterday evening, yet she's right there for Jean, and she's baking and training and putting everyone before herself."

As I listened, I attempted not to think of a goblin eating the Paris-Brest I was tucking into a box. Boy, was I

strung out. I needed to forget my dreams and focus on Alice. I'd been working way too hard on my folklore research. It would do me good to take a break and forget about everything that went bump in the night. Fat chance of that.

"She infuriates me," Alice continued. It was pretty much the same every day. Inès had turned the management of the café over to Alice months ago, intending to step back, but she was struggling to let go. At least she was now training Guy to do the bread and José to do the patisserie, but Inès was still the sole viennoiserie proprietor—her yeast baked goods like croissants and brioche had to be perfect. That aside, it didn't help that Alice was on edge after her breakup with Florence last week.

"And," Alice added, "she looks weird. Has done since this morning. Her face is red... blotchy."

"Yep, I noticed. But she's almost finished for the day, right?"

Alice shrugged. "If she sticks to the plan." She put a payment through the till. "Oh, and before I forget, we have less staff tomorrow than I'd thought."

I did my best to restrain the grimace that was attempting to form. We'd been short-staffed all week due to winter-sickness bugs, and it had been crazy.

"I know, I know." She raised her hands then dealt with the next in line. "There's nothing I can do about it. Plus, I've got the dentist in the morning. I'll leave once you're here, so you're going to be really short for an hour. But I have to get this filling done. My tooth is agonising and it's

the only short-notice appointment they had." Her brow rose in pitiful apology.

I bumped her arm before turning away to make a load of espressos. "Come on, Alice, it'll be fine. You have to get that tooth done." She still looked overwrought. "And give it a few more days. The staff will be back, and things will return to normal."

The corner of her mouth curved up wistfully. "The staff will return, Maman will put her feet up, and... spring will arrive."

I smiled. "Exactly. And look at that." I inclined my head to the queue that had shrunk to one person, Doctor Fournier. "The rush is over."

She nodded, taking a deep breath. "Thanks for the pep talk."

"Makes a change. You're usually the one giving me advice."

She grinned, then her face fell. Inès headed behind the counter, making a beeline for the kitchen. Her cheeks were ruddy, her eyes dull.

"I'll be back in a minute," Alice said. "I'm going to order Maman home. She looks worse."

"Hello, Camille." The doctor's keen eyes glittered as he stepped up to the counter, the waves of his grey head bobbing as he transferred his medical bag to his other hand and rummaged in his pocket for his wallet. "I'd like an espresso to drink in and a croquembouche to take with me when I leave, if you please. I'm celebrating."

I blanched at the mention of the ogre, the horrific

image returning much too clearly. The croquembouche shared its name with one of France's most popular desserts, a heaped tower of chouquettes—small golden puff pastries, their middles filled with cream. The dessert could be served in a variety of ways, but the café's version was sprinkled with powdered sugar and drizzled with chocolate that hardened into indulgent strands. The two shared the same name because "croquembouche" meant "something that crunches in the mouth". Ogres liked to crunch children as a tasty snack, and mere mortals liked chouquettes. There was a kind of grim logic in there.

"Sure thing," I said, trying to push away the impression of a horrendous mouth dripping with saliva as I shuffled a magnificent croquembouche from the glass-fronted chilled counter into a specially designed box. Damn it. I needed to get a grip. I placed the box back in the chiller and wrote the doctor's name on the top, all ready for when he'd finished his coffee.

"Let me guess why you're celebrating." I tapped in his order. "You've found someone to take over your practice?"

His eyes shone. "Got it in one. The fifth interviewee, and he's perfect. We're sorting out the finer details, but I don't think there will be any problems."

I turned to the machine and made his espresso. "Sounds like you'll be retiring on time, then." I glanced back as I waited for the coffee. The doctor was beaming, his joviality infectious, chasing away thoughts of ogres and goblins.

"First of May," he said, "I'll be passing on the keys to

the consulting room, if everything goes according to plan. There will be a brief handover period, then plenty of time to take the camper around Europe for the summer."

"Sounds perfect." I set the espresso on the counter. The D&D guys pushed through the door and huddled behind the doctor. "But I'm going to miss you," I added as he paid. And I really would. I couldn't imagine how anyone would fill his shoes. He was the town's only doctor and he'd been a rock. A reliable and sensible voice amidst small-town politics that could so easily turn petty, not to mention a supportive doctor, always available.

"I'm sure the new chap will more than make up for my retirement." He picked up his espresso. "I'm in absolutely no doubt of that. His qualifications are extraordinary, and just from our brief meeting, I could tell he has a superb bedside manner. Anyway, I'll still be around—in between plenty of vacations, that is." He turned away and headed to a table.

Félix the dungeon master took his place before the till, his frame tall and stocky for a teen. Gabe stood next to him, dressed as an elf, as usual. The rest of the gang lurked behind. Their coats and Gabe's cloak were dusted with snow.

Félix brushed back his caramel curls and cleared his throat. "High Warrior of the Borders: Protector and Holder of the Knowledge of Free Men and Fae," he proclaimed in my general direction.

I stared at him. "What did you call me?"

"Uh... High Warrior of the Borders: Protector and

Holder of the Knowledge of Free Men and Fae," he repeated, this time a little uncertainly. The rest of the gang tittered behind him.

"Where did you get that one from?" Gabe asked. "That new campaign you're working on?"

"I don't know," Félix stammered. "I... uh... it just popped into my head when I saw Camille."

I laughed. "Well, it's not the worst thing I've been called." And that was the truth. "Although I'm not sure I'm quite up to the job."

Félix grinned. "I don't know, I think you're pretty kickass."

Bless him, that was so sweet. Possibly based on the fact that I could handle a sword. Grampi had introduced me to swordplay when I was young, and I loved it. Even though we only fought with blunted blades, I guessed it was reasonably impressive to any fantasy nerd. Of course, he didn't realise that on the rare occasion I nicked someone and drew blood, I almost fainted—I was such a mess with that sort of thing. Anyway, it hardly ever happened thanks to the control I'd built over the years and the mass of armour we wore at tournaments, and it was a small detail he didn't need to know. I put on my best smile. "I'll attempt to live up to my reputation."

Raised voices came from the kitchen. I tried to ignore them. "Anyway, what can I get you guys?" One ear caught a yell of "Get some damned rest" from Alice, and a shout of "Don't tell me what to do" from Inès.

The gang and the closest clientele peered in the direc-

tion of the ruckus, then Félix gathered himself. "Four hot chocolates to go."

I started their order. Alice stormed in and joined me at the machine, tears in her eyes. "I don't know what to do with her," she muttered. "She won't listen, she won't even take a break in the office, and she looks like hell—"

"Alice!" Guy yelled from the kitchen. "Get in here now!"

Alice sprinted back in. I abandoned the hot chocolates and followed.

Guy knelt on the floor next to Inès.

Chapter 3

Alice dove down. "Maman!" she cried.

Inès's eyelids fluttered.

"I'll get help." My heart thrashing, every part of me willing Inès to be alright, I ran out and called for Doctor Fournier, the D&D guys looking on with worried faces. The doctor rushed behind the counter, bag in hand, and followed me into the kitchen.

By the time we got there, Inès was sitting up, her expression woozy, Alice's arm around her shoulder. My heart slowed a little. She was okay.

"I'm fine," Inès said as the doctor approached. "It's nothing at all, just one of my faints."

He crouched down and took her pulse. "Come now, Inès. Don't give me that. It's plain for everyone to see, you've been working too hard again." He strapped on an old-style blood pressure monitor and puffed it up.

"Don't *you* give me that, Hector," Inès snapped. "I'm

perfectly capable of doing a day's work." Alice rolled her eyes. The poor girl. Her mother had caused her so much worry. If only Inès would accept her limits.

"Yes," the doctor replied as he took her temperature, "but doing weeks without a break is entirely another thing, especially with your chronic fatigue. You're no good to anyone sprawled on the floor. Your temperature is raised and I'm ordering you to go home and rest up for a few days. If not, well, you could quite possibly have the beginnings of the bug that's going around, and I'm sure Health and Safety would be interested to hear that you may be contagious and yet you're still preparing food."

"You wouldn't dare." She glowered at him.

He shrugged. "Are you going to take that risk?" That would do it. Inès would do anything to preserve the reputation of the café.

"Come on, Maman." Alice squeezed her shoulders. "I'm taking you home."

"We'll be fine here," I said. Truth be told, with one more hand down, it would be a nightmare, but we'd manage.

"Yep, all good," Guy added, brushing his blond mop out of his eyes. "It's only clearing up in here, anyway."

With Alice and Guy's help, Inès rose slowly to her feet.

"I'll pop by later to check you're alright," the doctor said. "For now, complete bed rest."

As Alice and Inès shuffled past, I placed my hand on Alice's arm. "Text me to let me know she's okay."

"Sure will," she replied.

I returned to the counter and finished the D&D guys' hot chocolates, a glimmer of the croquembouche returning on the edge of my vision as if summoned by my worry for Inès, and with it a deep chill leached through my bones. The sensation continued as I drove home at the end of my manic shift, checked on Grampi in the farmhouse, then hauled myself through the snowy yard to my loft apartment above the barn. Exhausted, I fell straight into bed.

Blackness surrounded me.

"Honestly, gov. Is fancy dress really necessary?" a gruff voice mumbled quietly. "After all, she's not going to remember much of this anyway, and this get-up is making me sneeze. Of all the costumes. Me and the Men look like overstuffed pompoms. It's not exactly our usual aesthetic."

"She won't remember much," another voice murmured, this one low and honeyed and decisive, even in its hushed tone. "But something might stick, so best we keep the disguises. If she doesn't get the job, we don't want her remembering me here, or remembering you at all. Does Fickleturn have the creatures ready?"

"All set and raring to go. Not that he's happy about working with you."

I shifted, wondering why there were people in my bedroom.

"I think she's waking," the honeyed voice said.

"Shall we start the suffocating?" the other one asked.

"May as well get on with it."

The blackness I'd taken for a dark room pressed in, fur and fluff filling my eyes, my nostrils, my mouth. Something pushed down on my chest, stealing my breath. Panic tightened my throat. I flailed and struggled to sit up, but the blackness held me, a thick, smothering blanket. I grabbed at it, trying to yank off whatever pinned me down, grasping soft fur and flinging it away.

"Ouch," it cried. "This is definitely not in the job description." But as soon as I'd pulled one lot off, more covered me. If I didn't do something, I would suffocate.

With everything I could muster, I rolled against the fur and turned over onto my hands and knees, creating a small cave where my body arced over the bed. I gasped for breath, fur pressing in from the sides. But I wasn't kneeling on the bed. My knees scraped against a hard surface. Before I could be engulfed again, I forced myself up, flinging off the fur.

I blinked. I stood in a circular chamber, arched and unglazed windows all about. Ivy and roses trailed everywhere and bright moonlight shone in, glinting off the leaves. Around my feet swarmed a mass of black, cat-like things, yet not quite cats. Their fur was so fluffy that it radiated out in massive pompoms, legs, eyes and noses barely prominent. Sarra-maucas—they had to be—folkloric creatures that sat on the chests of victims, suffocating them in their sleep, just as they'd attempted on me.

"Not sure we was of much use there, boss," one of

them muttered. "We're not cut out for attacking innocent victims. Guilty victims is another matter completely."

Had I seen that right? The little black fluffy kitty-ball of evil had spoken. Not possible. It attempted a sneer. If I didn't know better, I'd say it was trying to look tough and menacing, but failing abysmally. But, it struck me, sarra-maucas didn't exist. Plus, I was standing in a phantasmagorical room. I was dreaming.

Pretty good dream, though. Everything was clear and very real. I followed the sarra-maucas as they padded away and gathered around the feet of a figure that leant against the wall, his arms folded across his chest. His eyes glimmered from behind a black masquerade mask. Beneath, his angled face was intriguing, the lips of his broad mouth pressing together smugly.

Dreams. One minute I was being smothered by cats, the next, I'd conjured up a well-developed, lithe and stunningly attractive man. Albeit one wearing long boots, breeches, a shirt with a ruff and a tailcoat. But despite the appeal, I had the impression that something else lurked beneath the surface. Something dangerous. Something that would be the death of me.

"Camille Amiel." He drew my name out slowly as he stepped over then paused before me, his gaze scrutinising, an intense curiosity in what I could see of his eyes. The awareness of my body grew with his gaze. I glanced down at myself, certain I was wearing unusual clothes. A sort of soft leather covered me in tight, medieval-ish trousers and a top. Pretty neat, especially the boots. They were solid

and comfortable, yet they clung to my calves in just the right way.

"It's a pleasure to finally meet you," the man added, his straight, tousled hair shifting in the slight breeze.

I watched the play of his lips, beguiled by the movement, but the back of my neck prickled. I had to admit, I was both ridiculously attracted to him and at the same time completely repelled. What warped aspect of my subconscious had created this guy? I hauled up my gaze to meet his eyes. Something to do with the mask messed with my head. "What's going on?" I said. "Who are you?"

"Someone who is wondering what sort of a person you are..." he murmured. "What sort of a person might become so much a part of my life..."

"What?"

He stepped back and gestured around the turret. "This is your job interview, and I'm your appraiser."

I laughed. "Job interview? What kind of job?" So now I didn't just have to work all day, my dreams were insisting I work all night too. Wonderful.

"The job of High Warrior of the Borders: Protector and Holder of the Knowledge of Free Men and Fae, of course," he said with a smirk. "It's a silly title and not remotely accurate, but it will do for our purposes." I stared at him. It was what Félix had called me today. My daily life was being processed by my exhausted brain. But I had to hand it to myself, the dream was so damned lucid. I turned around to see if I was completely in control of my actions. Yep, I was one hundred percent in command of

myself. It was an intriguing feeling. "And what does the job entail?" I asked.

"That will be explained if you qualify for the position. For now, get your bearings. Fae is a little different to the human realm."

"Fae, huh?" That was the second time he'd mentioned it. "This is turning into a humdinger of a dream."

"It's not a dream," he replied. "As I said, it's a job interview. We've merely hijacked your dreams to bring a part of you to Fae for the trial."

I walked over to the nearest window, by which stood a brass telescope. Leaning against the stone sill, I peered out. A huge full moon hung in the clear sky, illuminating a massive medieval chateau sprawled below. We were standing in one of its conical turrets. Beneath, crenellated walkways lay on the roof of a keep that held countless arched windows. There were stairs too, at the far end. Trees supported the lower parts of the structure, their trunks and boughs part of the architecture. Vines trailed everywhere, weaving around grotesques and gargoyles, giving the chateau the appearance that it was part of nature itself. And it definitely wasn't winter—the breeze was pleasant.

Far below, in the midst of the chateau, stood a massive courtyard. In its centre rose a dais surrounded by greenery. Something lay atop. I couldn't make out what it was, but it drew me.

"Take a look." The man gestured to the telescope.

I gazed through the bronze rim and adjusted the lens

until the courtyard came into focus. Upon the dais lay an unconscious figure, her grey hair bundled in a headscarf, her face much too pale. Inès.

As I watched, a black mist rolled in, surrounding her on three sides. I peered at it, absorbed by its darkness. Even though I was nowhere near the thing, I could feel its chill. It was a maloumbro, a shadow of sickness, well known in local folklore for maddening animals and people, and for bringing death.

The certainty that Inès was in danger poured through me. If that thing touched her... if it engulfed her... there was no way she could survive. My blood ran cold, the sense of unease I'd felt all day deepening.

Chapter 4

I turned to the man. "Why is Inès here?"

"Inès is in grave danger." He spoke nonchalantly, his chin at an arrogant angle. "The maloumbro will engulf her, unless you release her from its grip. We've set up the little trial to see if you're up to the job, plus there are a few other tests along the way. Hopefully it should be fun."

"If she isn't completely traumatised in the process," the largest of the sarra-maucas added.

"You know," I said, "I don't like the way this dream is turning out. Sleep is most definitely for rest, not for traipsing about castles rescuing people. Inès is a projection of my daily worries, meaning I don't actually need to rescue anyone."

"But can you take that chance?" he asked.

I went still. I had the feeling that the thing around Inès was very real, and that she needed help. But it was just a reflection of my anxieties. I was being ridiculous. "Yes, I

can completely take the risk. I need a rest. I need to be ready for a busy day at the café tomorrow. I'm not going rescuing."

"Told you she wouldn't play," the big sarra-mauca said, then it sneezed. "Bloody costume. I'm getting right itchy."

"What I'm going to do is stand here"—I propped myself against the wall—"and enjoy the lovely scenery that really is quite stunning. I'm going to relax until it's time to wake up." I didn't need to feed my apprehension.

"We'll see about that." The man glanced at one of the arches. "Crows," he called.

From the windows, in swooped hundreds of black wings. The crows dove at me, their feathers fluttering in my face, their cries piercing. I flung my arms around, fighting them off, doing little to stop beaks and claws tearing my skin. The man just stood there watching, conveniently crow-free himself.

"I honestly don't like this, gov," the big sarra-mauca said. "It's not like she's done anything wrong."

The man shrugged. "And what am I supposed to do about it? She has to have the test."

Only then did I register that there wasn't a door in the turret. As I fought off the crows, the window by the telescope remained bird-free. I ran for it. A little way below the turret was a defensive parapet that led along the edge of the keep to some stairs.

The crows continued their onslaught, blocking the rest of the turret. My only option was the vine that covered the outside of the tower. I straddled the ledge then clambered

out onto the branches, my head lowered against the flurry of wings, a beak slashing my arm.

Seeking secure foot and handholds, I scrambled down, the crows drawing back. Something nipped at my fingers, sharp pain lancing through the tips. I pulled a hand away and peered closer. Hidden behind the vines were hundreds of brown moths with disproportionately large and very sharp teeth. One gnashed at my other hand. I scurried down the rest of the vine and hurtled back against the far wall of the parapet, my chest heaving. The foliage looked beautiful in the moonlight, but ugh, no.

A shape moved up in the turret window. "Good luck, Camille," the man called, the last few crows perched on branches around him. "I mean that."

As I regained my breath, anger rose from my middle. "You set crows on me, and vicious moths, then you wish me luck. What the hell kind of a person are you?"

"Definitely a hellish kind of a person." He turned away.

Attempting to breathe through my irritation, I searched about for ideas. What I really wanted was to have a nice stroll through this curious place. Although if my experiences so far were anything to go by, that wouldn't be possible.

I turned to the parapets, my torn skin burning. Not wanting to be mauled by moths, I avoided the plants trailing everywhere as I gazed at Inès below. The maloumbro swirled around her, drawing in the enigmatic moonlight as though it was consuming all life, all hope.

One thing was for sure, Inès shouldn't be anywhere near it. I wanted to go to her, to see why she was lying there like that, to help her away from the shadow, but this was only a dream.

Beyond the chateau's moonlit walls lay another world. All I could make out was forest in every direction, inky in the half-light, and a silver river curling into the distance. Well, best I follow where the dream led and let it play out. It would end somewhere—or hopefully morph into something nicer.

I made my way along the parapets. The place was eerie. Beautiful, yes, but unnerving, as though something would jump out of the shadows at any moment. The parapet led to a dark doorway and stairs. I stepped downward, spiralling gradually. The courtyard and Inès were always visible through arched windows to my side, the way lit by moonlight.

When the stairs ended, I was about halfway to the ground, the keep walls looming outside. I followed the corridor, ducking under honeysuckle twines and trailing bryony. Not far along, a side passage led off from the arches. I paused, wondering which way to go. But it seemed sensible to head along the main thoroughfare.

I descended again, trotting down steps until I entered another corridor, this time not far from the base. The vines that clung to one of the arches shifted, and I almost sprang into the air. It hadn't been a vine. A small grey goblin sat against the side of the arch, dressed in a tunic and ragged breeches. His

bulging eyes studied the moth he pincered between gnarled fingers. His pointed ears twitched and the tufts of hair on his gaunt head wavered. The moth fluttered in desperation.

"Camille Amiel," he said, glancing at me. "How terrible and not at all interesting to meet you."

I stepped back. I really had been doing too much research. Even Shroom-Jean's goblin had made it into my dreams.

"It's absolutely ridiculous," he continued, "that I've had to help out with this... that I'm having to work with the arrogant, good-for-nothing..." He seemed to reconsider his words. "No matter. I have a couple of lovely surprises lined up for you, and I suppose it will be mildly entertaining to see how you fare. Especially as certain death is guaranteed." He flicked the now lifeless moth out of the window.

"Challenges? What challenges? I really don't need any more crows."

"Oh, no. I promise you they will be much worse than that." He glanced along the corridor.

I followed his gaze. From a dark archway at the end stomped something I'd hoped with all my heart I'd never, ever have to meet. It was hulking and muscly, yet its thin black skin was drawn tight over its bulk. It had beady eyes, slits for a nose and a massive, almost circular mouth with more teeth than one creature should have to clean—although I was sure dental hygiene wasn't its priority. It lumbered toward me on stumpy legs, its brawny arms

dangling low, its needle-tipped nails scratching the flagstones.

"Croquembouche," I muttered, stepping backward as it shuffled closer. My heart thrashed, cold sweat beading on my skin. Alice and I had been seven when one of the older kids at school had told us about the ogre that lived behind old Monsieur Babault's fence, about how it would pounce on us when we passed, and how if we were naughty it would hide under our beds and eat us as we slept.

We would run at full pelt past Monsieur Babault's property, and we'd so desperately tried to be good. That had failed miserably, so we'd lived in abject terror, waiting for it to come and get us. I'd had nightmares for months. They'd been so bad that Maman and Papa had taken me to Doctor Fournier, who'd put it down to passing childhood anxiety. I guessed he'd been right, because my fears had eased. But now, that same cold white terror dripped through me.

The ogre advanced, only strides away. I was going to die. But that was silly... I could run. I spun around, but the vines that hugged the walls had twisted inward, forming a barrier across the corridor. I clawed at them, scattering moths that nipped my face as they swarmed.

The croquembouche shifted closer. The windows—I could get out there. As I ran over, the cackling goblin skittered away along the corridor behind the monster. Before I could reach the sill, leafy tendrils closed in, blocking all escape.

I turned to the croquembouche. As it neared, its mouth grew wider, filling its face, its eyes disappearing. Still growing, its maw encompassed its neck, then its chest, until the beast was nothing but a single massive mouth, its stinking, rotten breath choking me.

Its jaws drew over my head. Panic taking hold, I flailed and kicked, only managing to skewer myself on razor-sharp teeth. The entire creature engulfed me, and my body streaked with agony as its teeth chomped my flesh.

Chapter 5

I forced myself to sit up, my breath heaving, the sensation of the croquembouche's teeth still much too vivid. I was drenched in sweat and my head spun. The familiar surroundings of my loft came into focus—the kitchen at the far end and the living area with the French windows that looked out onto the farm and Tarascon beyond. I'd had a dream, a nightmare, that was all. I flung myself back, drawing the duvet tight. Then it struck me... daylight... it was light outside. Damn it, I was late for work again, and Alice had her dentist appointment...

I grabbed my phone. The alarm had gone off ages ago. I'd slept through. Faster than I'd ever thought possible, I tugged on my clothes and outdoor things then stomped through the night's snowfall to the truck.

Grampi was crossing the goat-filled yard, wads of straw in his arms.

"See you later," I called.

"Plenty of milk this morning," he hollered as I climbed in. He was fine, and I'd check in on him properly when I got back. I pelted to the café much too fast for my snow chains. Once parked up, I slunk inside and shrugged off my coat as I headed to the counter.

Alice stood at the till. I caught her eye, expecting anger. It would've been appropriate. She'd missed her appointment at the dentist—without me, there wouldn't have been enough staff to cover. On top of Inès being sick, I'd put her under even more stress and pain.

But what I saw in her face was concern, then exhaustion. Shit. I couldn't believe I'd let her down. She meant so much... What's more, I didn't want to risk our friendship by being a terrible employee. She needed support right now, not me oversleeping.

"I'm sorry," I said as I passed her on the way to stash my things in the rear. Once I'd done that, then secured my apron and hair, I went back in and started making up orders.

"I missed the dentist." She didn't look at me as she tallied up at the till.

"I don't know what to say..."

She handed a bundle of patisserie to a customer, then turned to me, studying my face. "I'm worried, Camille."

I raised an eyebrow.

"About you. You've looked terrible the past few days, and you keep being late. I mean, I know you have the odd hungover morning, and there was that time you didn't even turn up after that bender when someone drove you to

Venice and left you on a gondolier." Not my best moment, I'd admit. "But it's not like you on a daily basis."

"I know, I know." I shook my head. "I've not been sleeping well, having bad dreams, that sort of thing. I slept through my alarm." The croquembouche came to mind, ice running down my spine. "But I really am alright. I'm just so pissed you missed your appointment."

She shrugged. "Oh, and remember, I have to go to the cash and carry tomorrow morning. You're holding fort until I get back at lunchtime. And can you pick up the milk on the way? There's a problem at the dairy and they don't think they'll be able to deliver until after opening."

"Yep, sure thing." How could I forget about tomorrow? She was trusting me with supervising the whole show for a few hours. After this morning, I wouldn't be surprised if she'd changed her mind.

Doctor Fournier strode up to the counter.

"How can I help you?" Alice said. The thought of his order yesterday brought the croquembouche back once more. I felt sick... sick with myself for letting Alice down, and sick with unease at the prospect of having to sleep tonight and face that thing. But hey, I might not dream of it again. I stepped away and tidied the patisserie display.

"An espresso please, Alice," the doctor said. "How is Inès doing?"

She brewed his order. "She's feverish. Doctor Fournier, I'm worried about her."

He studied Alice for a moment. "I have a house call in

a few minutes, but I'll check in on her after that and see how she's doing. That should put your mind to rest."

She nodded. "Thanks. I'd appreciate it."

He picked up his coffee and headed to his table.

Alice joined me at the chiller. "Honestly, I'm so worried about Maman. She doesn't look right, and I've got all this worry building in me... I'm focussing on work, on anything other than the worry just to get through."

"Oh, Alice." I wrapped my arms around her. She sobbed into my neck, her body trembling. And I'd made things worse for her today. "I didn't realise it was getting to you quite this much. I'm so sorry for this morning."

She pulled back. "I know."

Guy approached, his fuzzy blond mop dishevelled as usual, a large dollop of dough on his nose. Despite everything, I couldn't help laughing. Alice guffawed and shook her head. "There's nothing like humour to chase away worries."

"What?" Guy said as he passed.

"Nothing," we replied in unison, trying to keep straight faces.

I clasped Alice's hands in mine and swung them, just as I had when we were little. "Look, Inès needs time to let go of everything she's built up here." I glanced around at the café. "But she's one tough woman. I know she'll be fine." As I said it, I saw her laid out on the dais in the chateau courtyard, the maloumbro surrounding her. For some ridiculous reason, I couldn't shake the notion that she wasn't fine at all.

The rest of the day was a blur. We were rushed off our feet, customers complaining because there wasn't any viennoiserie—Inès's speciality. To Alice's relief and mine, she managed to scrape a late appointment at the dentist's due to a cancellation. But all through the afternoon, my unease grew, and the café, usually bright and warm, pressed in, dark and oppressive. The apprehension gnawing at my chest was almost unbearable. When I finally made it home, I was too tired and anxious to eat anything. I gazed at my still-unmade bed. It was ridiculous. I was a grown woman, not a seven-year-old with a fear of what went bump in the night. But no matter how I tried to reason it out, I didn't want to go to sleep. I ended up watching Netflix, the hours trickling past.

Chapter 6

Darkness encompassed me. Fluff pressed in on all sides and weight bore down on my chest.

Not this again.

I struggled against the sarra-maucas to no avail. Deciding on yesterday's tactic, I turned over, managed to get leverage, and pushed myself up to standing. The sarra-maucas dropped to the ground with thuds—not at all like slinky cats. "Sorry, miss," one of them muttered. "Didn't mean to cause you any discomfort."

"And smothering me isn't going to do that?" I growled, brushing kitty fur off my warrior outfit. At least dream me had a very stylish though slightly outlandish taste in clothes. I took in my surroundings. Same tower, same moonlight, same masked tormentor.

"Surely sarra-maucas are preferable to being eaten by a croquembouche," the man said lightly, the corners of his mouth twitching. "That really was quite entertaining. It

looks as though our challenges will be a little too much for you."

I glared at him. "What am I doing back here? Yes, I've been eaten, and I can tell you, it wasn't a whole lot of fun, but the dream ended. I didn't help Inès. I failed your interview dismally. So we're finished, and you can disappear out of my head once and for all."

He grinned. "Unfortunately, that's not possible. Inès is still in danger, and you are the only one who can help."

I rushed over to the window with the telescope and gazed out. The maloumbro had grown, I was sure of it. I grabbed the telescope and peered through. Yep. The black shadow had closed in on her, covering her partially. I turned back. "I don't want to do this. I want to wake up."

He studied me with that gaze I couldn't quite fathom, with a scrutiny that was too intense. He was an enigma in a mask. "This is not a normal dream. If Inès is devoured by the maloumbro, she won't survive."

"And you're just going to stand there, all dressed up with nowhere to go, while I have to battle creatures from hell and rescue my friend's mother?" I glowered at him.

He adjusted his ruff. "Exactly. And if you don't get on with it, I hate to think what will happen. That maloumbro looks hungry."

Shaking my head, I leant out the window again. I couldn't accept that I was having a job interview, and I definitely couldn't accept that I was in Fae, but as I peered at Inès, I knew she was in danger. Yet how could I help her when the croquembouche stood in my path? I thought

back to the previous dream. There had been a side passage —another option. But what else lay in wait? Shivers ran through me, though the sensation was nothing compared to the chill that encroached on Inès.

"Hold the crows," I said as I climbed over the windowsill, batting at the vines. The moths fluttered out in a cloud and disappeared into the night. I lowered myself from branch to branch until my feet met stone, then I ran along the parapet and took the stairs.

It wasn't until halfway down the keep where the passage led off the main corridor that I paused, swallowing at the thought of the croquembouche ahead. At least I had an alternative route. I stepped into the passage.

The walls were lit with torches that hung on the only patches of stone without greenery. Plants trailed everywhere else—hydrangeas, honeysuckle, germander. As I continued on, the foliage became finer, the vines thinner with thorns protruding from the stems. Amidst the dark leaves, black roses bloomed, deep rosettes swollen with countless petals, the scent rich and intoxicating. Ahead lay a dead end, and a cruciform shape glinted on the end wall. As I stepped forward, the shape became clear, a sword. Just what I needed. There was no way through, but my subconscious had provided me with my weapon of choice to deal with the croquembouche, thank you very much.

I ran onward, but as I did so, the scent grew thick and cloying. I struggled for air, my lungs prickling, the walls spinning. There was something about the fragrance... It was poisoning me. Clamping my mouth shut, I sprinted

back up the passageway to the main corridor and dove to the window, gasping in the cool night air.

Shit. I had to be more careful in this place. I peered down to the courtyard, searching for other ideas. I could see Inès clearly from here, the maloumbro swirling about. There had to be something I could do. Climbing down the vines wasn't an option as there were areas of wall devoid of plant life.

Nope, I needed that sword. I had to figure out how to get past the noxious fragrance. But then, the first rose bushes hadn't been that far from the dead end. All I'd need to do was hold my breath, run, take the sword and get the hell out of there. There could be some other trickery lying in wait, but as far as I could see, there were no alternatives.

I took another deep breath of fresh air, then entered the passageway once again. As the hydrangeas and ivy trailed away and thorned rose stems covered the walls, I stopped and drew deep breaths. Sweat beaded on my brow, my muscles tightening. If I wasn't careful, I was going to lose my nerve. Thinking of Inès, I drew a last, massive breath then pelted along the corridor, pulled the sword from the wall and turned back. But a gauzy form rose before me, the soft outlines of a delicate face shimmering, a slender chiffon body shifting this way and that as though undulating on an invisible breeze. A sylph—an elemental spirit of the air. The unnerving anxiety I'd carried with me lessened a little with her presence.

"Camille," she called, her voice gusty. "I know you're

in a hurry, but I'm here to help." I needed all the help I could get, and I could hold my breath a bit longer. I placed my hand over my mouth and shook my head in what I hoped was a clear sign for *I can't speak or breathe because the room is filled with an intoxicating aroma that obviously isn't affecting you.*

She nodded. "I'll be brief. Not everyone likes your appraiser. Some would even go as far as to help you if it made his life a little harder." She raised her hand. In her fingers hung a silver key on a white ribbon. "You'll need this if you are to have any chance of success. Take it with the blessings of Naïs."

I wanted to ask who Naïs was, and why my interviewer wasn't liked, and who the hell he was anyway, but my chest panged. I'd need air very soon. I nodded my appreciation as I took the key, then I darted back the way I'd come. But before me, a thick barrier of thorns was closing in, the stems weaving into spiny layers.

Not again—not now. This place was evil. My chest bursting, I gripped the sword in both hands and hacked at the roses, cutting through the first layer. But the exertion made my need to breathe so much worse. I couldn't hold on any longer. Unable to resist, I drew in a deep gasp of toxic air, agony tearing through my lungs. I dropped the sword and the key and fell to the ground.

Chapter 7

I woke to the sound of my phone ringing. Not the awful, buzzing, maximum-volume alarm I'd set up last night, but Alice's ringtone. I glanced at the screen. Shit. The alarm had gone off ages ago, I'd missed three calls from Guy, and I was extremely late. Shit. Shit. Shit.

I answered. "Alice, I'm so, so sorry."

"Honestly, Camille, I don't know whether to be freakishly worried or completely furious. I've just had a call from Guy. You've not showed with the milk. He'd already tried you, apparently, but you weren't picking up." She sucked in a long breath. "The café will be open in five, there's no milk, and you're supposed to be supervising."

"I'm sorry, I'm so sorry," I repeated as I pulled on my jeans, fully aware of how lame I sounded and how I had nothing in my defence. "I'll pick up the milk and be there in no time. I'm going to put the phone down now so I can

get out of here, and you can bollock me in full later. But once again, I am so sorry."

She sighed. "Alright. But Camille, are you sure you're okay?"

Now I had her really worried. "Honestly, Alice, I'm fine. I'll get on top of it, I promise. I'm going now..." I disconnected, finished dressing and grabbed my things.

Damn it, I was such a shit friend, and an absolutely terrible employee. I had to sort myself out.

I let out a long breath as I made up a plate of brioche goûter. It was the café's signature dish, the light brioche wrapped around sticks of home-made dark chocolate, served with crème fraîche and strawberries. With the lunch rush finished, the kitchen was quiet, and Guy and José were handling orders at the till.

It had been hectic all morning because I'd had to do the first-thing preps as I'd worked, and because Alice hadn't returned after her trip to the cash and carry. She'd popped in to check on her mother, and Inès had been worse. Barely coherent, Alice had said. An image of the maloumbro encircling Inès flickered before me for the millionth time. Apparently Doctor Fournier would be over soon, and Alice would let me know what was going on.

Not only the maloumbro, but other images from my dreams plagued me—sylphs, crows, black roses, the croquembouche, the masked man. And yesterday's anxiety

had morphed into an overwhelming sense of dread. It was made worse by me reliving my two dismal endings again and again. No matter what I did, I couldn't let the images or the dread go. Perhaps I had to admit there might be something wrong with me.

The goûter finished, I carried it out with Shroom-Jean's coffee and headed to the fireplace where he'd managed to snag the cosiest armchair once again. When he'd come in, I'd told him work was too hectic for me to take a break today. His face had fallen, underlining that I really didn't have a handle on things at the moment, and that it wasn't only affecting me, it was affecting everyone else as well.

"I'm sorry, Jean, for dragging you all the way here in the blizzard." I set the brioche goûter down, jolting him from whatever planet he'd been on. "I'd love to hear your stories, but it's been frantic."

"Not to worry, not to worry," he muttered, peering in delight at the goûter I'd stacked with extra strawberries, extra crème fraîche, extra everything, to make up for the letdown. "I was going to tell you more about the goblin," he said. "We've covered most of Granny's stories, I thought you might be interested to hear a few of mine."

I narrowed my eyes. "What do you mean, a few of yours?"

"Oh, well, I've had a goblin hanging around recently, and it's caused me no end of trouble. The little blighter had my tools everywhere, he let the dogs out in the night,

he put out the range, and he spoiled my store of pumpkins, made them all go rotten."

Curious. Jean was attributing problems in his home to the same make-believe causation his grandmother had used. Folklore lived on.

"Course, I knew how to get the better of him, thanks to Granny," he said conspiratorially. "One night, I hid in the pantry, the door open a crack as I waited for him to dampen the range—he did that a lot. When I saw him creeping across the tiles on tiptoes, a mean glare on his wrinkly face, I sprang out, wrestled him to the ground and pulled off his trousers."

My mouth fell open. This wasn't folklore living on, it was a full-blown hallucination. Jean had been at the shrooms again, or this was the result of dropping acid years ago. Whatever the cause, it meant that everything I'd gleaned from Jean, every recollection of his childhood, was most likely a creation of his drug-addled brain.

Damn it. Damn it so damned hard. I'd been worried about this from the start, but his stories had seemed solid. What a complete and utter idiot I'd been. It was all just one giant trip.

"The trousers are the thing," Jean continued. "Once you have a goblin's trousers, you have power over them. Not a jerkin, not a coat, or a teeny scarf if they have one—it won't work. What you need is the trousers. Then they'll do anything for you. I've got my little chap chopping wood as we speak. Mind you, just because you can control their

actions, it doesn't mean you can control their speech. My critter cusses like a trooper all day long."

I nodded dumbly, then turned away as he tucked into a strawberry. What an utter folkloric fail.

As I headed over to the counter, my phone rang. Alice. "Hey," I answered, entering the office for privacy. "How's Inès?"

"Not good." Alice's voice trembled. "Camille, she's unconscious... in a coma. They took her to University Hospital Toulouse by ambulance and she's in the ICU." She sobbed. "They don't know what's wrong with her. They're doing tests, but they won't know anything for sure until the morning."

"Oh, hell," I muttered, my sense of dread deepening, every fibre of my being hoping desperately that Inès would be alright. I wanted to wrap my arms around Alice and give her whatever support I could. "What can I do? Come to the hospital?"

"No, no," she murmured. "I mean, yes, of course I want you here. But there's no one else who can hold fort at the café. Anyway, I've got family keeping me company. Believe me, they're more than enough."

"Sure." I knew that made sense. Inès didn't have a partner—Alice's dad had left the scene when she was little. But Alice had a load of aunts and uncles, though they were probably stressing her out rather than comforting her.

"I've got a meeting with the consultant in the morning for the test results," she added. "Can you be there for that?

I'm so worried about what they might find, and we've got more staff on then."

"Completely. Anything. In the meantime, just call me if you need me, and keep me updated."

"Will do."

"And stay strong," I said. "I know Inès will be okay. I'm sending you a massive hug."

"Thanks, Camille," she managed.

I disconnected and leant back against the filing cabinet, staring at the year calendar on the other side of the room, but not really seeing it. Inès was in serious trouble. Last night's dream spooled through my head again... It was ridiculous, but I had the overwhelming sense that I could help Inès... that I could save her. I just had to find a way past the roses, then I could take the croquembouche down with the sword.

But what else lay in wait...? I shuddered then laughed dryly at myself. Was this my way of coping with someone I loved being seriously ill—crusading in a dream? Even so, I couldn't shake the unwavering certainty that if I didn't do something, Inès would die.

I spend the rest of the afternoon thinking the dream over and planning how not to perish in agony. I grew increasingly jumpy at the thought of the croquembouche, springing into the air when Guy placed his hand on my shoulder. Alice called with an update later on, but there was no change, and they still didn't know what was wrong.

Eventually, I returned home. I was much too worried to eat. What I needed was to fall asleep and go help Inès. I

let Grampi know I was having an early night so he wouldn't disturb me. I was going to ask him to wake me in the morning, then remembered tomorrow he'd be selling his goat's cheese at the market in Toulouse. His friend would be along shortly to pick him up and he'd stay the night there, ready for the early start. So I set alarm after alarm on my phone, all different ringtones, and I found an old alarm clock and set that too. I had to be there for Alice in the morning.

After checking in with her again, I showered, undressed, tucked myself into bed and closed my eyes. I waited and waited for sleep to descend, tossing and turning, the bed growing hot and uncomfortable. At midnight I flung myself up and made a hot chocolate, cursing at my inability to sleep and hoping that the warm milk would settle me.

Chapter 8

Fur filled my mouth and weight pressed down on my chest.

"Get off me," I growled.

There were mutters of "Sorry there, miss" and "Excuse the, umm... paws." The sarra-maucas jumped off and I sprang up.

I was back in the tower again, as expected. My eyes lingered on the fine figure of the man as he quirked his lips, about to say something. Then I darted to the window, grabbed the telescope and checked Inès. The maloumbro covered her almost entirely. Only a small gap in the billowing darkness remained, Inès's arm and the edge of her body just visible. I could feel the shadow's chill, its lifelessness, and I knew, without a doubt, I had to get her away from it.

I scrambled out of the window and down the tower, moving too quickly for the moths to bite. With a burst of

speed, I ran along the parapet, descended the stairs to the side passage and paused before the black roses, the sword glinting on the far wall. The sylph could have been a ruse to delay me, to give the roses an opportunity to barricade the passage. Or had she truly been trying to help? If she was there again, I couldn't risk not taking the key if it might be of use. And if I didn't get to Inès... well, I wasn't sure there would be another chance.

My body trembling with the prospect of another awful demise, I hauled in deep breaths and held the last, then bolted along the passage, passing the sylph, who dangled the key from an outstretched hand. "So sorry about last time," she called. "I had no idea what that scoundrel had planned."

I grabbed the sword and sped back up the passage. The roses had already closed in, almost completely covering the exit. I snatched the key from the sylph's hand without slowing and ran for the thorns. The stems had interlocked, although the barrier wasn't yet thick and layered like yesterday. My chest tightened as I hacked at it, slicing through stem after stem, my lungs on fire. A few more slashes and I'd made a gap, then a hole big enough to squeeze through, but the tendrils continued unfurling. I chopped at them, then forced myself through the hole. Thorns ripped my clothes and tore my skin, but I was through.

I pelted along the corridor, my head spinning with lack of oxygen, my chest screaming that I had to breathe, yet I hung on. It wasn't until I'd passed the roses that, still

running, I gasped a massive breath. I sped to the closest window and flung myself over the side, hauling breath after breath, desperate for fresh air.

I'd done it. As my breath slowed, I turned and slid to the floor, my back against the wall, my body slackening with relief. The sword fell from my grip but the ribbon with the ornate silver key was caught around my fingers. I untangled the ribbon, looped it over my head and tucked the key inside my top.

After a few more moments of recovery, I grasped the sword and studied it. A standard medieval blade, well made and sharp, although lighter than typical. The perfect weapon to pay back a croquembouche. But… I was a wet blanket when it came to blood, and I'd never done worse than accidental minor damage with a blade. Would I be able to kill the croquembouche? If I didn't, the blasted thing would eat me. That was incentive enough. And Inès… I glanced at the dais below. The maloumbro had grown. I could only see a glimpse of Inès's clothes amidst the encroaching mist. There was no time to sit around.

I sprinted along the corridor and hammered down the stairs, spiralling around the central courtyard. Finally, I drew to a walk where the goblin sat in the window, jabbering to himself. And there, lumbering through the arch at the other end of the corridor, was the croquembouche.

I raised my blade ready to strike, but torn croquem-bouche limbs, a slashed head and way too much blood and gore swam before my eyes, the images dizzying me.

"Camille, get a grip," I muttered, my sword hand trembling—and I hadn't even broken flesh yet. Despite my imminent death, I wasn't sure I could cut the monster down. But the goblin had said he'd arranged the challenges for me. If he'd arranged the whole thing, he could unarrange it.

As the croquembouche trudged along the corridor, I darted to the side and grabbed the goblin. "Aaargh," he screeched as I wrestled him to the floor and sat on him. The thing was remarkably strong, despite the fact he was about half my size and much scrawnier.

I drew my blade to his throat. "Stop the croquembouche. Now."

He cackled. "Can't do that, Camille. Once it's out it won't stop until it's had a tasty snack, or until you've defeated it. One or the other." As the croquembouche stomped closer, I pressed the blade into the goblin. A bead of blue blood trickled from his neck. I gagged, the chateau swaying. I wasn't cut out for this. "It doesn't matter if you kill me," the goblin jabbered. "The croquembouche won't stop."

"Damn it," I cried, jumping off the goblin and flinging him to the side. I raised my blade once more, hoping the sight of it might deter the monster, but on it came, one thud of a step after another, its mouth growing wider, its breath reeking from here.

Terror flooded through my body. This was it. I'd be eaten again and I'd fail Inès. The ogre was almost upon me. Would it swallow the sword as well? Or would it use

the point as a toothpick for the pieces of Camille it would have to extract from its teeth? As terrified as I was, I couldn't help laughing. It wasn't a normal laugh, it was hysterical—fear and horror mingled with the utter ridiculousness of a giant mouth about to break my bones. It came out as a snigger, a chortle of insanity. The croquembouche paused and its mouth closed in, the whole creature shrinking ever so slightly.

I gaped at it, and something Alice mentioned at the café came back. "There's nothing like humour to chase away fears," she'd said when Guy had walked past with a dollop of dough on his nose. But that was it... The ogre was feeding on my fear.

The croquembouche's jaws expanded and it stepped forward again. I tried to think of something that might possibly be funny about an ogre eating me, and came up with absolutely nothing. But then... the croquembouche... the dessert... the huge pile of cream puffs. This thing, this massive lumbering beast, bulged as though it was stuffed with cream. For a split second it looked like a huge dessert, its dark skin a slathering of chocolate. I guffawed at the ridiculousness of the idea, and the monster deflated, its mouth narrowing.

That was it... The ogre was no more than a walking pile of choux pastry with teeth. My fear sank away and the croquembouche shrank again. It was powerless. I didn't even have to see it as patisserie to laugh. It was a petty monster that preyed on the fear of little kids. It was absolutely nothing.

The croquembouche shrank and disappeared. I stared at the stones on which it had stood, not quite able to believe I'd defeated it.

Clapping broke my reverie. The goblin was applauding slowly. "My, my, my. Camille Amiel managed to defeat the big bad ogre. How clever of her. Though I'm not sure she'll fare so well against my next challenge." He glanced out of the window. I followed his gaze to see Inès completely covered by the maloumbro.

Chapter 9

I pelted along the corridor and descended more steps. Passages led off here and there, but I followed the main thoroughfare downward. At the bottom, the stairs widened and swept outward beside the courtyard.

Pausing, I assessed the place. Huge Corinthian pillars rose up amidst equally massive tree trunks. Leafy boughs hung all about with fairy-creature grotesques protruding from the foliage, and the voluptuous full moon shone above, the turret looming before it. Something moved in one of the arched windows further down. The goblin was watching.

In the middle of the courtyard stood a broad circular platform with steps leading up, and in its centre the maloumbro churned. It almost hurt to look at the thing, to try to comprehend what it was. Rather than a something, it was a nothing. Coldness radiated from it, coldness and despair. Its presence deadened my insides, and I wanted to

curl up into a lifeless heap. Fighting hopelessness, I struggled to stay focussed. Inès couldn't survive in that.

I couldn't see any alternative than to run into the thing and pull her out. Heart thrashing, blood thrumming in my veins, I sprinted toward the platform and sprang up the first step, smashing into something and flying back onto hard stone. My breath sucked from me and I gasped for air.

Every part of me throbbed from the impact as I pushed myself up. I'd hit something. I reached out with my blade to where the step rose. Metal struck glass... but strange glass. I couldn't see a hint of my reflection or a glimmer of moonlight in it. I tapped higher and lower, then to the sides. An invisible barrier extended all around Inès and the maloumbro. I drew my blade back and swung it at the glass. The thunk shook my bones, and the surface remained undamaged. I swung at it again. Still nothing.

I strode around the circumference of the platform, constantly tapping at the barrier to check it was continuous. At the back, a small iron lock lay embedded in the glass where it met the step. I pulled the ribbon over my head, inserted the key and turned. The air shimmered. I tapped my sword again, and this time it met only a chill draught. A grin pulled at my lips. The sylph *had* been of help.

With the barrier down, the air grew colder, the hopelessness intensifying. I had to get through the maloumbro to pull Inès out. As I sized it up, the mist unfurled, and a curl of darkness touched my skin, stinging it with cold.

With a cut of my blade, I severed the tendril from the mass. The maloumbro seethed—it really hadn't liked that—then it roiled and burst toward me. I sliced at it, doing nothing but breaking up fragments of cloud that drifted back to their origin. The maloumbro coiled around my body, so damned freezing that I gasped, the blood draining out of me, my skin burning with cold.

I swiped again and again, but it crept closer. All I could do was edge away. Then it swelled forward. I had no choice but to run. The entrance with the stairs was, as far as I could see, the only escape route. I bolted for it, bitter mist billowing after me.

Having gained a little headway, I paused at the stairs. Damn it, I'd come this far. I had to figure out a way to get to Inès. One thing was for sure, I couldn't run through the maloumbro. But there had to be a solution—there had been a solution to all the previous problems, just not what I'd expected.

The mist encroached and I careened back up the stairs. Up was a million times worse than down, and my chest heaved. It became harder and harder to force my legs on, and still the maloumbro came. Finally, I entered the corridor where I'd defeated the croquembouche. The goblin was still in the arch.

"You," I cried. He'd set this up. He'd set the croquembouche on me, and the maloumbro, although I had the niggling feeling that the masked man was probably behind all of it. I charged for the critter again.

He looked as though he was considering jumping out

of the window to climb up the outside of the chateau, but before he could decide, I grabbed him and slammed him to the ground. The maloumbro swirled in at the end of the corridor.

"You little tyrant," I said, my blade once again at his throat. "Do something with the maloumbro, or we're both going to die."

He cackled. "Doesn't work like that. I've got special immunity as I'm not part of the interview."

"What about Inès? Does she have immunity?"

"Oh no." He cackled again. "The maloumbro has her firmly in its grasp, here and in the human realm."

"But you can do something," I yelled.

"But I won't, I won't, I won't," he screeched, flinching as I yanked his jerkin tight around his throat. The mist rolled in along the corridor. "Poor little Camille," he jabbered. "Looks like you're going to freeze to death as well as being asphyxiated and having your bones crunched. I have to admit, it's terribly amusing watching you die in multiple ways."

The mist slunk closer. Shit. I had to think of something... there had to be a shred of information that could help in all the folklore I'd researched... something about the maloumbro... or goblins... Then it clicked. What had Shroom-Jean said? If you take a goblin's trousers you gain control over it. But Jean had been tripping. Even so, there were accounts of humans obtaining power over fairies by stealing a garment of clothing.

I thrust my palm onto the goblin's chest, pinning him

down as I grabbed the waistband of his breeches. "No, not the trousers!" he squealed.

I yanked them off, balled them in my fist, and released him. "Stop the maloumbro. Now!"

The goblin glared at me as he hopped to the other side of the corridor and pressed a stone. A small door sprang open in the wall, a torch burning inside. He produced a taper from nowhere and lit the end, his scrawny hand trembling.

Muttering under his breath, he stepped toward the dark mist that was almost upon us, holding the glowing taper as far from his body as he could as though he didn't want it near him. "Blasted toadstools, I hope you rot with worms and toads and maggots," he said as he walked closer. When he reached the mist, the maloumbro retreated from the taper as if stung. It was afraid of fire... or light... or heat. Maybe all three.

I followed the goblin down the stairs, the maloumbro retreating, relief pouring through me. "Thank you, Shroom-Jean," I muttered. "I'll never doubt you again."

The mist crept all the way down, recoiling from the flame until, finally, it billowed backward into the courtyard. The goblin continued his advance, cussing terribly, and the maloumbro withdrew to the platform. As the goblin took the steps, the darkness stole further back, revealing the stone dais and Inès's deathly white body surrounded by leafless vines. Next to her stood a large iron brazier, small twigs stacked in its base, broken branches and logs above.

"Rotting slug guts and putrid cockroach brains," the goblin muttered as he approached the brazier. "Why the assembly thought I was appropriate for the job only shows what dull-witted morons they are." As he neared, his hand and the taper shook violently. "Nooooooo," he cried. His eyes bulged even more than normal. He was scared of something... but what? Maybe the maloumbro, but he'd been trembling ever since he'd lit the flame. He brought his hand to the brazier, shaking so violently he dropped the taper.

I gasped, my gaze darting to the maloumbro, but the taper remained lit and the mist held its position. Before the goblin could pick it up, I shoved the breeches into my sword hand, grabbed the taper and thrust the flame into the twigs at the bottom of the brazier. In seconds a blaze rose, engulfing the logs. Light and warmth filled the courtyard, and the maloumbro evaporated away.

The vines that surrounded Inès burst into leaf. I stepped over, propped my sword against the dais and tucked the breeches under my arm, then gathered her hand into mine. At first her skin was cold, then colour returned to her cheeks and her hand warmed. Desperate relief flooded through me, my legs shaking. The maloumbro was gone, and I knew deep within me that Inès was going to be okay.

The goblin was still standing by the roaring brazier, his face horror-struck as he gazed at the flames. "You little rotter," I snarled. "You left her to that cold hell of a mist, not to mention everything else." I raised my blade. I

wanted to chop off his scrawny head or skewer his chest. But come on, I almost fainted at a paper cut.

He glowered, glancing from me to the breeches in my hand. "You think I want to spend my time setting creatures from the dark lands on you? Believe me, I don't. I was forced into it. If you want to take it up with anyone, try him." I followed his gaze to the masked man, who leant against the vaulted entrance, looking more gorgeous than any man had a right to. The goblin had a point. The masked man was my appraiser—he'd forced me through the test.

I bent down to the goblin's level and waggled the breeches before him. "Tie him up," I whispered.

The goblin snorted repeatedly. I thought he was going to choke, but just possibly it could have been a laugh. He stepped away from the brazier and headed to the opposite side of the courtyard, well away from the man. Perhaps the trouser thing wasn't working. The critter clasped hold of a vine, and although it was difficult to see, he appeared to be whispering to it.

"Fickleturn, you little creep," came a cry from behind. I spun around. Vines had encircled the masked man, securing his ankles, wrists, middle and neck against the wall. Perfect.

"My absolute pleasure," the creature screeched. "Not that I had much choice in the matter."

I strode toward the man, blade in one hand, breeches in the other, anger burning through me. Halting before him, I drew the point of the sword to his neck. He could

barely move a muscle—only his fingers bunched and released.

"What kind of a sick, despicable, loathsome beast would raid someone's dreams and subject them to crows, moths with very big teeth, noxious roses, a croquembouche and a maloumbro?" I seethed. "Not to mention, you used Inès. You put her in danger just to test me." It occurred to me again that he was probably some warped part of my psyche. Even so, he needed dealing with.

He raised his chin and snickered. I followed the angle of his cheekbone to where it met his mask, the play of the laughter line below, the way the corner of his mouth drew up. The mask hid too much. What danger lay beneath? His irises were dark... so dark, studying me in return.

"I didn't use Inès," he said, his lips levelling. "She was gravely ill. You saved her. The obstacles you encountered were representations of barriers that truly lay around her."

I laughed. "People don't get ill from maloumbros, because maloumbros don't exist."

"Not everything is as straightforward as it might appear," he replied. "Disease can take many forms."

"And all in the name of a job interview." I scoffed. "What on earth makes you think I'd take a job that involves anything like the creatures here?"

"Because you're intrigued," he said. "About me, about the creatures, about fae."

"I'm as intrigued as I was that time I dreamt the president ate the espresso machine. It's just a dream."

"But you knew you had to save Inès…" He waggled his fingers as though the vines were restricting his blood flow.

"It was dream logic." I shook my head. But despite everything, I couldn't resist asking, "So, did I pass? Did I meet the requirements for whatever ridiculous job involves outsmarting fae?" Although after rescuing Inès, I couldn't see how I'd failed.

His eyes narrowed as he considered me for longer than was comfortable. "I never expected you to get past the croquembouche," he murmured softly. "I'm fascinated… What part of you complements me…? What part of me complements you…?" I had no idea what he was muttering about. Then he laughed again. "I think you're more than suited to the role, even though you had a little help with the key."

Still, he studied me. Somehow, he'd known about Inès, my love of swordplay and my fear of the croquembouche. He knew way too much about me. It would be good to level the playing field.

I placed the sword against the opposite wall. He wasn't a danger tied up, and the goblin, Fickleturn, wasn't a risk—he stood waiting for my next order. Stuffing the breeches into my pocket, I stepped close, examining the roughness of the man's stubble and the scar that ran down his neck to disappear under his ruff. As if he was drawing me, distracting me from what I'd been going to do, I moved closer still, unable to prevent myself absorbing his rosemary and cedar scent, unable to resist listening as he

released one light breath after another. He beguiled me. But it was the mask, that was all.

Something jostled my pocket. The man's fingers had reached from their bonds and tugged out the breeches.

"Fickleturn, release me," he cried. In the blink of an eye, he was free.

Darting back, I grabbed my blade and positioned it at his neck once more. He didn't know I wouldn't use it. His hands rose in surrender. "I believe you're fully aware," he drawled, waving the breeches, "that I can make Fickleturn do anything with these?"

I shook my head, my brow raised. "The moment you utter a word, I'll run my blade through your throat." Then in one fluid movement, I lowered the sword and sprang forward to make him think I wanted the breeches. He snatched them away, parting his lips to command the goblin, but before he could speak, I drew up my hand and pulled off his mask.

The chateau fell away and darkness descended. Soft words murmured in my head, "I will reveal myself to you, Camille. But not yet. When we meet in the human realm soon, I promise to show you exactly who I am."

Chapter 10

I flung myself upright.

Alice.

Half dazed, I scrambled out of bed and studied my phone, not quite able to believe what shone on the screen. It was half an hour before my alarm. I'd woken in time. Despite the end of my dream, I could only hope that Inès really was alright.

I cancelled the many alarms and clicked off the button on the old clock, then with trembling fingers, I texted Alice. No reply. That wasn't a good sign. But whatever was going on, I could be there early. I dressed as quickly as possible, then jumped in the truck and headed through the still-dark and snowy town to join the autoroute toward Toulouse. The hospital was about an hour away and, fretting that Alice still hadn't responded, I took the toll route for speed, then pushed the old truck to its limits, willing it to go faster.

It was silly, really. Alice probably just hadn't checked her phone, and I wasn't even sure she would be back at the hospital. She'd been intending to spend the night with an aunt, although she'd wanted to stay by Inès's side. Knowing Alice, she would've slept in the waiting room if they'd let her. And yet Inès had been so sick...

When I entered Toulouse, I met early commuter jams. There was nothing I could do but stop-start and check my phone repeatedly. Dawn broke with shafts of amber glossing the pristine sky. The weather front that had caused recent blizzards was gone, and when I cracked the window, I was certain there was a hint of mildness about the air. Finally, the modern industrial areas and offices of the outskirts morphed into the rosy townhouses of the old city. A few more minutes and I was crossing Pont Neuf, the hospital visible beyond the flowing waters of the Garonne. I drew into the sprawling complex, found the ICU, parked and ran in.

"Inès Roger, please," I said to the receptionist.

"It's not visiting time yet," she replied, her voice clipped.

"I'm a friend of her daughter's. She's not been answering her phone. She's been shaken by her mother's illness, and I need to check she's alright."

"Umm..." She checked the computer screen. "That patient... well, you better head up there. Second floor, ward five."

What did she mean? Inès couldn't have passed away—she couldn't have. I sprinted to the lift, ascended two floors

and found the ward, almost missing the turning. I was buzzed through into the waiting area, which lay empty. "Inès Roger?" I asked at the ward desk.

"Third room on the left," a nurse instructed.

I stepped to the door, my pace slowing, my heart thudding as I wondered what I would find inside. Surely the nurse would've let me know if something had happened to Inès. My stomach somersaulted as I peered around the door.

Inès was raised up just a little in bed. She was fully conscious, though covered in tubes and wires. She managed a small smile. Alice was sitting next to her. When she noticed me, she jumped up and rushed over, enveloping me in a hug. "Maman's alright," she murmured into my hair. "It was touch and go last night. The doctors had no idea what was happening so they let me stay. At one point we almost lost her..." She released a huge sob and pulled back. "Anyway, I'll tell you about that later. But the short version is, she came round from her coma a couple of hours ago. No one knows what happened, but she appears to be perfectly fine—much better than anyone in her condition should be. The doctors are keeping a close eye, but they're happy with how she's doing."

I wrapped my arms around her again, relief flooding through me. "I'm so glad," I muttered over and over. "I can't imagine what you've been through... I tried to text."

"Sorry." She squeezed me tighter. "I haven't a clue where I left my phone. Probably in my bag on silent. I've just been so..."

"No need to explain." It was completely understandable. And it only mattered that Inès was alright and by extension, Alice was too. At least she would be once she'd recovered from the shock of it all.

Finally we drew apart and Alice studied me. "You look better than you have for the past few days."

"I'm good. Just messed-up sleep patterns and the weirdest dreams. I..." I'd been going to go into more detail, as though my nightmares had been on the tip of my tongue, but I couldn't grasp the memory. "Just bad dreams," I said. "But I think they're over now." I had no idea why I had that impression, but I sort of felt at peace. Only the vague notion that a croquembouche had been involved remained. And weirdly, the unease, the remnant of childhood fear I'd always retained for the ogre, was gone.

Alice stepped over to Inès and settled in the seat next to her. I followed, pulling a chair alongside and sitting down. Even though Inès appeared a bit groggy, she had colour. She just looked alright. Her lips curved into that warm, familiar smile as she met my eye. "I'm glad you came," she said softly. "Seems like I've given everyone quite the scare."

I took her fingers gently into mine. "I have to say, you really did. I'm so relieved you're better."

"Me too, me too," she murmured. Then her smile broadened a little. "Camille. I wanted to say thank you."

I narrowed my brow. Alice glanced at me, curiosity in her eyes.

"What on earth for?" I asked. It couldn't be for the café. I was a reasonable employee most of the time, but my efforts certainly weren't worth acknowledging, especially lately. Perhaps she was thanking me for my friendship with Alice.

"I don't actually know what for," Inès said. "But I just wanted to say it. Thank you."

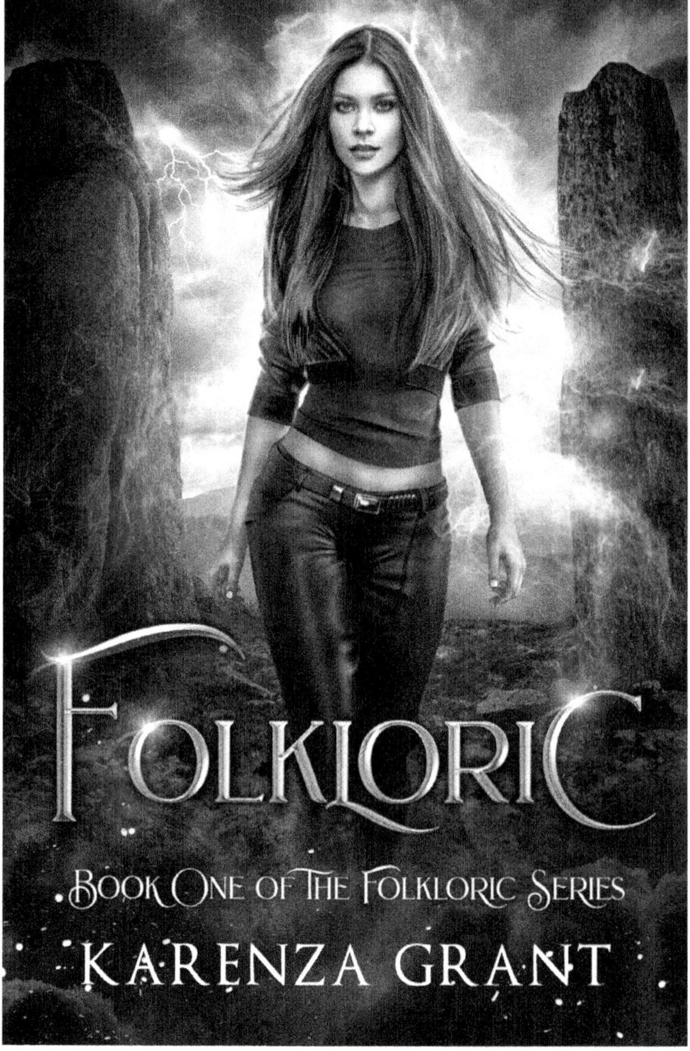
FOLKLORIC
BOOK ONE OF THE FOLKLORIC SERIES
KARENZA GRANT

Chapter 1

Folklore matters. Period.

It's not a load of old stories, done and dusted, or a lot of creepy tales to frighten kids, and it's definitely not some guy in authority choosing the latest version of history for the textbooks. It's the long-term memory of everyday people brought to life—it's the survival of everything *we* like to remember best.

Society couldn't function without folklore, and truth be told, I couldn't function without it either. It was my fascination, my obsession, the thing I loved most of all. Maybe it was my way of making small-town France and my even smaller life a little more interesting, or perhaps it was my method of understanding the world. In any case, it explained why after having just finished my exhausting shift at the café, I was still there, sitting opposite Tarascon's most odious jerk, attempting to get his story for my folklore research paper.

Max Legrand ran his fat fingers over his greasy face, palpating chubby cheeks beneath messy stubble. My phone lay on the table by Max's tea, voice record on.

"Well... I was coming around the side of the barn, helping Henri with a sack of feed." Max's voice filled the café from the beams in the vaulted ceiling to the cosy wood walls. The scent of his sweat spoiled the aroma of freshly baked bread. There was just too much of him—his width three times that of Henri sitting alongside, grinning in eagerness to hear the story again. Henri was always up for one of Max's recitations, although he was way too nice to be friends with the guy.

"And it was getting late," Max continued. "Dusk had settled and mist rolled in from the top of the mountain. I can tell you, it was a mite strange out there. I couldn't help looking over my shoulder. I'd call it eerie, I would."

Henri nodded enthusiastically, thinning hair bouncing above bright eyes. "Yep, it was some kind of eerie, alright."

"Yeah." Max's shirt buttons strained as he sat back and ran a hand over his buzz cut. "Eerie. Creepy, like." He grinned, peering around to make sure the room was listening. He wasn't telling this story for me, he was telling it for the attention.

Everyone stared at him, including the D&D geeks secluded away in their nook. They'd actually stopped rolling dice—a minor miracle as they made the most of every moment after school. Gabe, the lanky one who dressed as an elf, ear tips included, gawked at me. Félix the dungeon master and the others watched with peculiar

fascination, as though I was a lamb being led to the slaughter. Maybe they were right. With Max, anything was possible.

The town's new doctor sat opposite pretending not to listen, although casting the occasional glance in our direction. The rest of the café weren't being so subtle. They were on the edge of their seats.

I shifted, scraped back the espresso locks that had escaped my messy bun and attempted to loosen the apron tied tight over my jeans. I was much too hot in the late-May heat. Alice caught my eye from behind a counter stacked with the best patisserie for miles. She glared at me and shook her head, clearly code for "This guy is such a jerk. Don't waste your time". She was right, as always. She had that kind of sense that... made sense.

I focussed on Max. Boy, was he taking his time. "What happened then?" I pressed my lips together and nodded my encouragement.

Max sat back and narrowed his eyes. "Are you sure you want to hear this, Camille? I mean, it's just some stupid thing that happened the other day. It's not important, like."

The tease was clear in his eyes. It was important to me, and Max knew it. The research I'd amassed for my paper, *Recent Experiences of Ancient Folkloric Phenomena*, was rock solid. There was no way it wouldn't be published. I just needed a couple more case studies, and Max had been telling his cronies all week about a dark airborne figure he'd seen at Henri's.

I found it fascinating how people assigned paranormal origins to experiences they couldn't understand. There was always an explanation, of course. They just couldn't see it, so the paranormal stuck. Max truly believed his experience was real. And as much as I wanted to believe in monsters and fairies and everything in between, that kind of folklore sprang from the collective beliefs of the community.

The figure in Max's story was already being linked to the death of an old woman who'd lived nearby. She'd been ninety-seven and had died of old age, but it was intriguing how she'd become mixed up in this—the primeval fear of death rankling everyone. I got that—I hated death and dead things. But it was what shaped fear into story that interested me, and I needed a proper recording of Max's tale, rather than hearing second-hand snippets here and there.

"It would be extremely useful for my research, as you know." I fiddled with my necklace, chaining my fingers with silver then releasing them in an attempt not to show the tension creeping through me. "So I would be very grateful if you could continue." I was impressed with myself. I never sounded that patient.

He knocked back his tea. He'd be holed up in a bar if he didn't have to stay sober for driving his cab. Pyrenee's café was not his natural environment, but then, this was the second home to half the town. It was the cosy, take-your-time armchairs, and the brioche. Definitely the brioche.

"Oh, and I saw your grandfather the other day," he said.

I groaned inside. Here it came.

"He was talking about his goats, you know...?"

Don't respond, Camille. Don't respond.

"I heard old Delphine is missing," Henri put in. "She's been such a super queen to that herd. Did he manage to find her?"

"Nope, still missing," I said, distracted by the mischievous glint in Max's eye.

"Well, at least the old man can talk about *Delphine...*" Max laughed uproariously. "Can't talk about anything else. Mad as a hatter, that one. Good cheese, though."

The customers either shifted uneasily in their seats or snickered. I wanted to shout. I wanted to wring Max's neck and kick the sneer off his bloated lips whilst yelling that Grampi was one of the kindest, most decent people I knew. Way out of Max's league. But I wanted the story more, so I kept quiet, his words twisting me up.

For everyone else, Grampi *did* appear as mad as a hatter. The only thing that came out of his mouth were vague references to his herd of goats. Nothing else at all—ever—which made him a prime target for bullies like Max. But deep inside, he was one hundred percent compos mentis.

Not getting a rise, Max deflated. "Alright, now, where was I? Oh yes, the animal feed. And it was creepy out there—"

"And getting dark," Henri added.

Max nodded. "So, I'm carrying this sack of feed around the side of the barn, and I hear a sound. A kind of shrill wailing, and then a deep moaning born on the gale. Unearthly, I'd say. Not human, for sure."

This was really interesting. There had been many historic reports of evil creatures riding the wind to do mischief in the valley.

"It grew louder and louder," he continued, his eyes comically wide. "The shrieking piercing my ears, the atmosphere so damn bad I can't describe it, and the smell... like dead flesh rotted twenty times over."

And there were tales of fairy-like creatures only recognisable by their terrible odour. This fitted with two other local stories I'd collected. "And...?" I asked.

"By this time, I was rooted to the spot. And the wind grew, roaring around, whining through the barn. And then..." He paused dramatically, the café silent in anticipation. Gabe scratched his elf ear tip. It fell off and dropped into his cup.

"The boards of the little shed at the back shook like they'd be torn off the frame," Max boomed. "The screeching was coming from inside." He took a well-timed breath. Whatever else I thought of him, he was a master storyteller. "I didn't know what to do. I had a choice. Run away or confront the wailing." He puffed out his chest. "So I strode forward and threw open the shed door." Max glanced around at the expectant faces, then homed in on me. "And do you know what I saw, Camille?" he said in a theatrical whisper.

"Go on." Curiosity burned, despite myself.

"It was Henri!" Max raised his arms and gestured to the guy. "It was Henri on the john, groaning and wailing like nothing I'd heard before. He must have been in some pain." Max bellowed with laughter and slapped Henri on the back. The café broke out in howls. "Yep, that was it. Groaning like a good 'un, the poor lad."

Henri's mouth hung open for a moment, then he joined the uproar.

I stared at Max, unable to process what he'd said. Then it sank in. He'd made a joke of me and everything I loved, not to mention his opinions about Grampi. My insides twisted as anger spiked through me. He hadn't told me the real story—he'd been going on about a dark, ghostly figure all week. Was it really so difficult for him to tell me the same thing? He knew how much I wanted this.

I rose and snatched up my phone. "Max Legrand, you're a devious, conniving jerk who would rather get a laugh than help anybody." I leant toward him. "And one of these days, I'm going to pay you back for this so damned hard."

"Come on, Camille. I'm just having a jest." He ogled down my top. I flinched back. "I mean," he added, "it's not like you're one of them academics, or anything fancy like that. You're never going to get published, and you know it."

And there it was. The proverbial slap in my face, worse than his stupid joke, worse than his ogling, worse than anything else at all.

Chapter 2

I NEEDED TO GET OUT OF THERE—QUICKLY. BEFORE I did some serious harm to Max. But his words cut deep because they were true, and I couldn't deny it.

I headed behind the counter and into the corridor, pulled off my apron and found my bag. When I came back out, the café had returned to its usual chatter. Everyone had moved on, Max included, but not me.

Alice placed her hand on my arm. "He's not worth it. He's an ignorant troll who enjoys making fun of people—when he's not sexually harassing them."

Her warm eyes and round, sweet face peered out amidst her messy bob, the petals of her rose tattoo just visible on her collarbone. She was a comforting contrast to the intensity I saw in the mirror. "Everyone was laughing," I said. "Not just at Max's story. Laughing at my ridiculous attempts to do something serious with my research. As he said, I'm not an acad-

emic, and I never will be. My work won't be accepted."

"You know more about the folklore of the area than any old, balding scholar," she replied softly. "And I wasn't laughing."

I raised my brow. That wasn't enough.

"And the D&D guys, they weren't laughing," she tried. "And the doctor—he kept a straight face through all of it."

"Why were you looking in the doctor's direction?" I couldn't help the tease despite it all.

"Just admiring. Nothing more." She reached over and tucked an escaped strand of hair behind my ear, something she'd done since we were knee high. "Sweetie, you don't usually care about what people think. What's going on—?"

Someone cleared their throat from the other side of the counter. Félix the dungeon master stood there, all chubby, fluffy-teen cheeks and caramel curls. Gabe was next to him, the hood of his elven cloak drawn over his head, hiding his missing ear tip and casting his badly shaved deep-bronze skin into shade. The other two members of the team peered over their shoulders.

"Umm," Félix attempted, shifting uneasily. "We wanted to say that we honour and respect the High Warrior of the Borders: Protector and Holder of the Knowledge of Free Men and Fae." He meant me, his expression earnest. The others nodded in agreement.

For some unknown reason, they'd started addressing me like that a few months ago, and it always caught me off guard. They seemed to be my greatest fans. I guessed they

immortalised me in their game, which was more than a little creepy. It was probably because I knew my way around a sword, thanks to Grampi. Or perhaps on some deep level they detected I was a true nerd, just like them.

Félix scratched his nose. "And we think Max is a complete jerk."

"I... appreciate that, guys," I said, touched. "Thank you." But Max was still much too close, and I really couldn't be there any longer. "Gotta go," I said to Alice.

She tilted her chin, assessing me from the corner of her eye as she rewrapped the tie of her apron over her dungarees. "You going to be okay?"

"Of course." I pasted on a grin. But I was so completely far from fine. "I'm going to leave my truck and walk home. I need to clear my head." Letting her know meant she wouldn't worry about my abandoned vehicle in the car park. I kissed her on the cheek. "Love you."

Outside the back door, a bundle of rags huddled on the path, a messy beard and hawk nose just visible in its midst. Roux was sleeping off whatever he'd been drinking. Alice would be out soon with a coffee. He hated being disturbed for any other reason—when he was sober enough to notice.

I stepped quietly past and almost slid my foot into a bloody mess. A mangled mouse carcass lay on the path, its body torn, its features set with terror, its skull visible on one side.

"Damn it, Fifi," I muttered, fighting a retch and looking away, which did nothing to remove the images of

broken flesh strobing through my head. If only she wouldn't deposit lifeless bodies everywhere. It was hideous... revolting... like all dead things.

Roux grunted at the disturbance, and the rest of the world came back—the flank of Coustarous looming behind the café, its slopes bathed in the afternoon sun, the meadow below lush green.

It was always the same—my complete overreaction to death. Wounds and blood weren't too great either. And I really couldn't take it after Max and the café filled with laughter—laughter at my utter failure to achieve anything in life.

I needed something to ease the pain.

#

From my secluded corner at the back of Brasserie le Saint Roch, I peered out at the world, my hands wrapped protectively around my Bourbon, the bottle on the table emptying more quickly than was healthy.

The French doors that usually extended across the front of the bar had been drawn open to allow in the sun, and the traffic of the N20 thundered past—lorries of tomatoes from Spain, heading to Northern Europe on one of the few half-decent routes through the Pyrenees mountains.

Life strolled past on the pavement, shadows growing long as the evening progressed. A few customers stepped inside. The doctor had come in a half hour after me and was sitting at the front, gazing out. He was already a good

way down his second bottle of wine. Looked like I wasn't the only one with problems.

My idea was that if I got completely plastered, I would forget all about my research, the paper and Max's smug, conceited face. Things were getting fuzzy around the edges. It was working. If I kept at it, I wouldn't remember a thing, and tomorrow, I'd be too preoccupied coping with the hangover to care about anything else. Such a great plan and not at all self-destructive. Never say I didn't face my problems.

My phone buzzed again. Yet another text from Alice to check I was okay. I reassured her, but the inclusion of the straw-hat-with-a-little-bow emoji might have been a mistake. I'd meant to press the smiley.

Raised voices at the bar drew my attention. It was much better to tune in to someone else's life than think about mine. "And he was in Gourbit," the guy on the bar-stool said. "You know, that farm out the other side of the village."

"Know the place," Ren the barman replied gruffly as he polished a glass.

"Well, Max heard a wailing and a shrieking, some kind of demon born on the wind—"

I covered my ears and groaned as my failure rose up like that blasted demon and slapped me once again. "Forget. Forget. Forget. Forget. Forget," I murmured. When they appeared to have moved on to other things, I poured another shot and tipped it back, then poured again. The sweet, sweet liquid sank in, and my vision blurred some

more. Through the haze I made out the doctor heading over.

"Hey," he said as he walked past for the bathroom. I struggled to think of a response. *Hey to you too, my life is shit*, came to mind, but it didn't seem appropriate, so I attempted a smile that felt more like a wonky grimace. When he returned, he went to his table, gathered his bottle and glass, and stepped over. I wasn't sure if it was my vision or him, but he appeared to be swaying a little.

"Camille, isn't it?" he asked in a low voice. I could already tell he had a good bedside manner.

"Yep, that's me. Folklore research failure and butt of Max's jokes." A positive introduction always made a good impression.

He chuckled. "Mind if I join you?"

"Nope. Go ahead." I gestured to the empty chair, happy for any kind of distraction from... me.

"Can I get you a glass?" he said, placing the bottle down.

The thought of mixing wine with Bourbon flipped my stomach. "No, I'm good."

He settled at the table, his broad mouth slanted in a grin, his straight, swept-back hair a dark umber mess. As he studied me, his eyes narrowed, accentuating the angles in his face. I'd guess he was a few years older than me and, all in all, I could see what had caught Alice's eye. Truth be told, he'd already caught my attention too. A belch rose in my throat. I stifled it pretty well, though.

"So, Max is an asshole," he said.

I stared at him for a moment. I had the idea that doctors were honour bound not to insult their patients—with a code of ethics or something. Then it struck me that Max wasn't a conversation I wanted to be having. But I couldn't help the words escaping. "He's the most abysmal abomination of an absolute ass that ever stepped into this town." I took a mouthful of Bourbon, and actually, I kind of felt better for letting my irritation out.

"Yep." He took a sip of wine, turning his head. A scar ran from under his ear, disappearing into his open shirt collar. "That was pretty evident. The guy is a complete and utter jerk."

My lips tugged upwards. "Do all doctors talk like that?"

He shook his head, his face lit with something I couldn't put my finger on. Shrewdness, perhaps. "Only the ones who've had way too much to drink." Then his expression settled. "But I was wondering, earlier in the café... You're really into folklore, right?"

"Absolutely."

"Then, if you don't mind me asking, why don't you go study at uni or something?"

I had to laugh. "Going straight for the jugular? I would've thought Max had sent you if you'd not been so insulting about the guy." I'd wanted to shove every part of my life into a dumpster for the night, and now this. But confronting everything might do me good. Not my usual approach, but maybe it would help to talk the damned thing through.

I met his assessing gaze. "Well, I was going to. At least, I got as far as the interview for Toulouse. But the professor didn't appreciate my argument with his theories about the morphing of Pyrenean gods into Christian saints. He was clearly incorrect."

The doctor's lips drew together as if he was trying not to smile. Even so, the corners of his eyes creased.

"I wasn't going to put up with his rubbish," I continued, "and he didn't like that, so I didn't get the place. But you know, two years later"—I sat up and smirked—"my arguments were proven correct."

"I do know that," he replied.

"What? How? Very few people know anything about the subject—other than folklore nerds, of course."

He leant forward, his elbows on the table, his glass in his hands. "I, uh, have an interest in folklore."

I gawked at him. He'd just uttered the ultimate chat-up line of my dreams, the one I'd fantasised about a cute guy in a bar saying before... Well, let's not go there. His proximity brought the scent of cedar wood and maybe rosemary, the natural fragrance drawing me more than any overpriced, chemical rubbish. I shook myself, making the room sway.

I needed to get a grip. Talking about folklore was in no way suggestive to anyone in the world but me. Although his body language, leaning in as he was, did indicate a degree of interest. Damn. I was way too plastered to assess the situation properly.

"So why don't you apply to a new uni?" he added.

I glanced outside. Twilight was unfurling, the lights of the traffic too bright. "I chose to stick around and care for my grandfather when my parents moved away. They wanted to put him in a home, but he's completely functional apart from..."

"The goat thing?"

"Yep, the ol' goat thing." He needed a middleman for communication. And anyway, money was tight. The farm had endless bills.

I swirled my glass, spinning the Bourbon. In the years since I'd unsuccessfully applied for uni, I'd studied every aspect of local folklore I could get my hands on. I'd read every paper, I'd done piles of my own research. Now, I wasn't certain the lightweight syllabus of a degree taking three years of my time was worth it. But how else would I get acceptance as an academic?

"You know," he said, "I sometimes wonder if scholars in universities are the best people to record what belongs to a living population. It takes someone who knows the mountains, who feels the pulse of the valleys within them."

I studied him. My thoughts exactly. There was a case for the objective observer, but bringing in a researcher from outside a community always caused problems. He met my gaze, neither of us looking away. He really was hot, and it wasn't just the folklore. Then it dawned on my addled brain—he was a complete mystery. I didn't even know his first name. "You're Doctor Rouseau, right?"

"Sorry." He sat back and dragged his hands over his

face. "I think I left my manners behind with the fifth glass. It's Lucas. Lucas Rouseau."

"So, what's your story?" I asked. "What brings you in here nursing more than one bottle? Can't be much worse than having to deal with Max."

"It's bad. It's really bad." There was something grim in his eyes, then he broke into laughter. "I mean, we all have stuff, right? Work stuff, family stuff, life stuff. I guess it's just stuff."

An eloquent answer. I nodded. "The curse of stuff. It beats being a self-absorbed rejected folklorist."

He bit his lip then glanced at me. "You know that story of Max's—the real story, not the one with the john?"

"How could I not? Everyone is talking about it."

He wrapped both hands around his glass, his face serious, as though this was a grave moment. "It's real—the thing he saw. Completely real."

My lips pursed, a smile attempting to escape, but he appeared so solemn, I couldn't let it. "Yeah?" I managed, but the smile won. It broke its bounds and I guffawed.

His expression broke too, and he roared with laughter. "And hobgoblins—real too," he added, cracking up.

I loved his silliness and I wanted to play. "And sinagries—giant spectral dogs—you'd better watch out for them."

Ren came out from behind the bar and strode to our table. "Right, you two, there's no way you're driving home. Keys."

Lucas and I looked at each other and burst out

laughing again. I shifted for access to my pocket and had to grab the table to stop myself falling off the chair, stoking a new volley of giggles. Once I'd clambered back on, I just about managed to detach my car key from its ring, then I cast it onto the table. Lucas did the same. Ren gathered them up with a shake of his head. "I'm glad I'm not you two tomorrow morning," he said before retreating hastily.

"And elves, and gnomes, and dwarves, and dracs, and nymphs are all completely real." Lucas didn't miss a beat.

I snorted repeatedly, tears beading in the corners of my eyes. Lucas gathered himself, his lips stilling into a small smile. He drew his hand to mine and traced my knuckles in and out. His touch sent shivers through me, replacing the hilarity with something carnal.

I matched his gaze, and we grinned, then I turned my hand and took his fingers into mine, playing with his smooth skin. I liked this guy very much. Ha! I'd been right. Despite my inebriated state, I'd interpreted his flirting correctly. I mean, folklore, right? The ultimate chat-up line.

He raised his hand to my cheek, his thumb brushing my lower lip, his glance following as though he was having a hard time restraining himself.

"Oh, and unicorns... got to be so real," I said, relishing his attention.

"Yeah, but they're pretty rare. I've only seen one, and that was from a distance."

My eyes settled on his broad, straight mouth. "Okay. I have to admit, I don't know much about unicorns."

He drew up my chin so my eyes met his, his touch something else. "I can't show you a unicorn, but I know a way we can lose ourselves that will be even better than drink." His eyes sparkled, his gaze devouring me—a complete turn-on.

I ignored the voice screaming—no, caterwauling—*think of the morning*, and *he's the only doctor for miles. What about the next time you need medical assistance?* But that was stupid. I'd be fine. It was the perfect way for two adults to drown their problems.

I pulled out my phone to call a cab. "Your place or mine?"

The story continues in Folkloric...

Leaving a review...

Reviews make a big difference to me as an independent author. I don't have the financial muscle power of a New York publisher, but I do have something worth much more than that.

Wonderful readers!

Honest reviews help bring my book to the attention of other readers.

I would be hugely grateful if you could take a moment to leave a review (as short as you like) on the book's Amazon page. You can jump straight to the page with the QR code.

Thank you very much!

Afterword

It's been such a wild experience writing Folkloric—the series has given me so many laughs already, and I'm eager to venture into more antics.

I'm guessing some of you, if you're anything like me, like to embark on armchair voyages, googling locations, or perhaps you like to geek out on folklore. So here are a few notes on the setting and local mythology. After all, Camille would never forgive me if I didn't give you the lowdown.

Most of the series locations in the human realm exist. Tarascon (its full name is Tarascon-sur-Ariège) is a stunning town in the South of France, nestled in the Ariège valley in the foothills of the Pyrenees mountains. Despite its beauty, it's no tourist town. It's situated on one of the major routes through the mountains between France and Spain, and it's an industrial centre with quite a history.

I fell in love with the area at first sight. Forest-clad

mountains shelter the valley, castles perch high on remote crags, and caves descend far into the depths of the earth. The poetry and artistry of the troubadours that blossomed here in the 12th century laid the foundation for the novel as we know it, and way back in prehistoric times, the first modern humans (the Aurignacians) emerged here—the region is known as the cradle of civilisation. It's also a place associated with Arab invasion and Charlemagne, not to mention rebellion, heretic religions and the grail. As you can see, there is plenty of fuel for urban fantasy.

Above all, though, it bears a wildness and a mysterious otherness. It's not difficult to imagine other realms nearby —that an entrance might lie behind an old gnarled box tree or within a stalagmite-filled cavern. And it doesn't take much to envisage a fae town under the slopes of Coustarous.

As to the folklore, I try to draw as much as possible from the actual mythology of the region, and many of the creatures in the Folkloric series are noted in local lore. As in other places, it has its fair share of fae, goblins, trolls, dragons and giants. However, the specifics get very interesting. Think of dracs, the fae of Bédeilhac (known in Folkloric as the Men), Dame Blanche, the croquembouche, the hantaumo, Count Estruch, and many other examples—too many to mention here. Curiously, Count Estruch was a real count and the origin of the earliest European vampire myths. If you want to google what he got up to, be warned, it isn't pleasant.

The Pyrenees mountain range also has its own

pantheon of gods, ruled over by Abellion, a sun god akin to Apollo. Baeserte and Aherbelste are other examples. What very little is known about them has been obtained from roman excavations. Roman gods gradually replaced the old pantheon, and more recently, Christian saints supplanted the Roman deities. In spite of that, the traits of the old gods live on in more recent personifications, so there is something to be gleaned.

Having said all this, there's not a whole load of lore to go on for the purpose of creating characters. A couple of paragraphs on how dracs shift into gold cups, luring people to their watery graves, isn't much to shape into a wily doctor with rather mischievous tendencies. I have two words for you: artistic licence. Yet when I can stick to the lore, I do so.

If you want to find out more, there's not much published in English, although Martin Locker's *The Tears of Pyrene* is superb. If you read French, try one of Olivier de Marliave's excellent tomes on the subject, for example, *Trésor de la Mythology Pyrénéenne*.

Before I finish, there are a few people I'd like to mention who have been instrumental in getting this series off the ground. Octavia Denning, my gratitude to you is unending. Dorine Maine, thank you for everything from the bottom of my heart. A special shout-out goes to my writing group: Viktoria Dahill, Katie Mouallek, Rachel Cooper and Abhivyakti Singh, for always being honest and saying what needs to be said. You keep me on my toes and striving to do my best. Jack Barrow and P.M. Gilbert,

it's been great working with you. Many thanks to Toby Selwyn, my super editor, and to Deranged Doctor Designs for the top-notch covers despite my terrible cover specs. I'm indebted to my superb ARC and Street Team. You guys rock. Massive thanks goes to L.A. McBride for answering question after question with angelic patience. Rillian Grant and Minerva Grant, you make it all worthwhile. And last of all, thanks to you, the intrepid reader, for daring to delve into this utterly crazy world.

About the Author

Karenza Grant writes fun and feisty urban fantasy with plenty of humour and a little sweet romance.

Her early years in Cornwall were largely the source of her fascination with all things mysterious. She lived below a hill reputed to be the Cornish residence of the Unseelie Court, and the local myths got their claws in. Now she's inspired by a broad range of creators from Jim Henson, Arthur Rackham, and Olivier de Marliave, to a whole host of amazing authors on the urban fantasy scene. Currently, she's enjoying weaving her love of France into page-turning stories.

She has three black cats known as The Three Guardians, and a crazy lab x spaniel who is just about the only thing that can extract Karenza from her writing desk—if the pooch isn't walked, the legions of hell will be released.

Connect

There's nothing better than hearing from readers. Drop me a line or join me on social media. I hang around on Facebook on a daily basis and would love to see you there.

You can find all the links on my website:
www.karenzagrant.com

Printed in Dunstable, United Kingdom

63744703R00068

13291098R00068

Printed in Great Britain
by Amazon.co.uk, Ltd.,
Marston Gate.

Albert Fish

«?Albert Fish 1903?». Sous licence Domaine public via Wikimedia Commons - http://commons.wikimedia.org/wiki/File:Albert_Fish_1903.JPG#/media/File:Albert_Fish_1903.JPG

Chikatilo

"Chikatilo-mugshot" by Rostov Police Department - Rostov Police Department photographic records.. Via Wikipedia - http://en.wikipedia.org/wiki/File:Chikatilo-mugshot.jpg#/media/File:Chikatilo-mugshot.jpg

Image credits

Luis Garavito

«?Luis Alfredo Garavito Cubillos?» par NaTaLiia0497 — Travail personnel. Sous licence CC BY-SA 3.0 via Wikimedia Commons - http://commons.wikimedia.org/wiki/File:Luis_Alfredo_Garavito_Cubillos.jpg#/media/File:Luis_Alfredo_Garavito_Cubillos.jpg

Amelia Dyer

"Amelia dyer1893" by Wells Asylum authorities, 1893 - Wells Asylum, 1893. Licensed under Public Domain via Wikimedia Commons - http://commons.wikimedia.org/wiki/File:Amelia_dyer1893.jpg#/media/File:Amelia_dyer1893.jpg

Richard Tenton Chase

"RichardTrentonChase" by Tahoe City Police Department - Tahoe City Police Department photographic records.. Via Wikipedia - http://en.wikipedia.org/wiki/File:RichardTrentonChase.JPG#/media/File:RichardTrentonChase.JPG

Robert Hansen

"Robert Hansen" by Alaskan Police Department - Alaskan Police Department. Via Wikipedia - http://en.wikipedia.org/wiki/File:Robert_Hansen.jpg#/media/File:Robert_Hansen.jpg

Sources and Image Credits

Sources

Berry-Dee, C. (2003). *Talking with serial killers*. London: John Blake.

Bonn, S. (n.d.). *Why we love serial killers*.

Bull, R. (2006). *Criminal psychology*. Oxford: Oneworld.

Crouch, B., Kilborn, J. and Konrath, J. (2011). *Serial killers uncut*. [S.l.: s.n.].

Greig, C. (2012). *Serial killers*. London: Arcturus.

Marsons, A. (n.d.). *Silent scream*.

Murray, W. (2008). *Serial killers*. U.K.: Canary Press.

Newton, M. (2006). *The encyclopedia of serial killers*. New York: Facts On File.

Philbin, T. and Philbin, M. (n.d.). *The Killer book of serial killers*.

Schechter, H. (2004). *The serial killer files*. New York: Ballantine Books.

Vronsky, P., Newton, M., Perrini, S., Ladwig, D. and Parker, R. (2014). *Serial killers true crime anthology*. Place of publication not identified: RJ Parker Publishing.

Wilson, C. and Seaman, D. (2007). *The serial killers*. London: Virgin.